COUNTDOWN

Countdown

Ashley Roberts

Countdown

Little Bit of Art Store

ISBN 979-8-9956558-0-0 (paperback)

ISBN 979-8-9956558-1-7 (ebook)

Printed in the United States of America

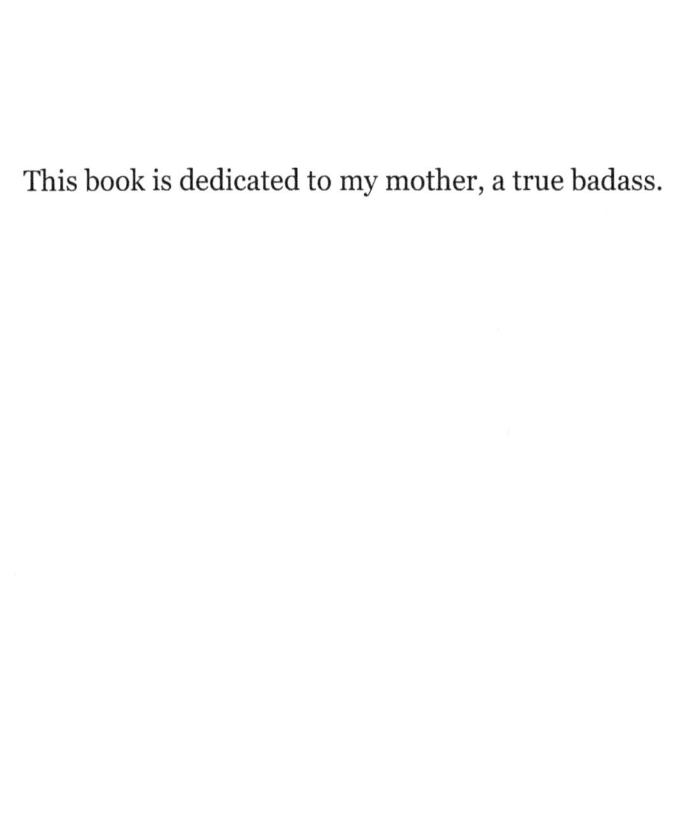

This book is dedicated to my mother, a true badass.

PREFACE

When I started this book, it was an outlet for my creativity while I was stuck in the Arizona Department of Environmental Quality office. Imagine saying that all day on the phone without going crazy. I always enjoyed writing but had never written anything long enough to contain a storyline . . . or had the time to. I felt my imagination ran wild with this idea of wishing fingers. It allowed me to de-stress in environments where emails thrived, phones rang, and tasks were time-constrained. I continued to write whenever possible as jobs and environments around me changed. This book has my heart in it, written by my very own fingers.

CHAPTER ONE

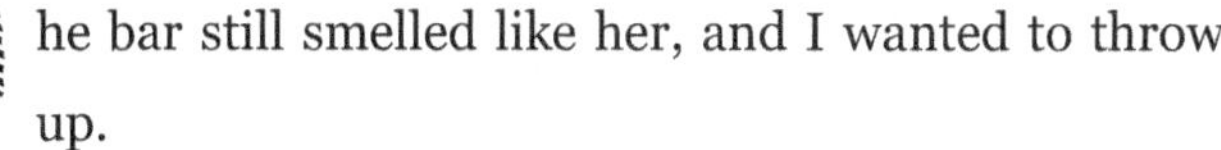

The bar still smelled like her, and I wanted to throw up.

A mix of mint, peanuts, and sweet whiskey filled the corners of my mind. After she'd get home, I'd take us to the movies. We'd watch a film, and she'd burn through a pack of cigarettes after ranting about how the movie got this wrong or that.

All of my senses recalled those days.

The soft graze of her hand on the back of mine. The way the smoke would flow out of her nose while she talked. How much I hated seeing the smoke engulf her. The slight wrinkle between her eyes would show itself when she hit the end of the cigarette. Under the street lamp's light behind the movie theater, she'd grab my hand to pull me away from our dark, safe corner to head back home, but I'd always drag my feet.

My hands were rough now, worn out from all the work I had to do. I didn't think she'd even want to grab my hand now; they'd changed too much, and I'd lost too many fingers.

I didn't have ten fingers.

Sitting at the bar with my whiskey on the rocks in my old hometown, I remembered when I could grasp something with such strength that it might crumble, missing the feelings of a life lost. Looking down at the appendages that touch the condensation produced by the ice in my glass, I was stuck with six. Life goes on; the people around me seemed like they couldn't care less. In the bar's silence, I debated how I'd come to have three on each hand. I was now more of an outcast than I was before. And alone.

I missed my middle right finger the most; I used it the most. But I could do without my pinky.

I could imagine the look you would give me if I reached out to you, eyes big and face wrinkling. A freakshow. Disgust. Confusion. Weirded out. Maybe you wouldn't even fucking care. Guess what, I don't care.

So how did I get here? I can start with the moment that changed everything—when a mysterious woman offered me a deal that seemed too strange to ignore.

What if you could have ten wishes but lose a finger with each one? It's a strange trade-off, but I'd do it, because I have.

If you are like me, you value the human body. You think it's exquisite despite all of its flaws. I grew up playing sports and discovering just how much the physical limits of a body could bend—fractures, sprains, bruised skin, and getting a leg broken after falling off the stage. However, despite my appreciation for the human form, I have never been much of an artist. Growing up was slow and painful, caught between my Mom and Dad as I tried to make something of my life. Met with the challenges of trying to fit in, I had a resident bully. I felt like I could never win. It's starting to sound like every other story out there, but trust me, this is different.

Life is tough shit, and sometimes you have to step in it.

Recently, my life has consisted of turning corners every day, holding the same damn floppy piece of garbage cardboard that says, "Too ugly to strip, God Bless." Getting forcefully leathered in the hot New Mexico sun, cars would pass me without a second glance. It has been a couple of years like this now. At least two, but I can never keep track of the time nowadays. I never planned on doing this; I gave up on many things and made terrible decisions. I took the bad luck and involved myself with the wrong people who promised more. I guess the rest is history.

So, sitting there in my corner one day and thinking about the taste of a peach—God, I can't remember the last time I had a peach—I had my thoughts interrupted.

A giant black Suburban pulls up to my corner. The hunk of junk was idling for a bit, but it stopped at the curb right before the light at the intersection. I put my small cardboard sign on the dirt and had a staring contest. Placing my hands on my hips, I squinted from the setting sun while locking in any movement from the car. I am always on high alert in situations like this; sometimes, people want to cause trouble. It was unmarked and spotless. I saw a silhouette through the tinted windows, and I imagined in my head what kind of bald motherfucker would emerge from it. But, as with any other assumption, I was very wrong. Out stepped the most beautiful woman I had ever seen in a brilliant, deep purple pant-suit. Her hair was glowing like white fire, and every part of her not covered by the suit was a canvas for the deepest reds. Awestruck, I sat there and let her clippy-cloppy heels walk up to me. It seemed as if she was floating towards me.

I knew she smelled like daybreak; she knew how to be a new person every day. Instinct told me I couldn't trust her. My days on the streets had proven that the only person you can trust is: fucking no one. So, I let her walk up to me, building my mental wall and furling my fingers into a fist: fight or flight.

"Are you Justin?" she said, but when she said it, I heard about five different voices at once.

Now this is some creepy shit, I thought.

I couldn't even think of a reply because people hadn't called me Justin in quite a while. I felt like I was being taken back to a different lifetime, one where Justin didn't fuck up and had to change his name to Albert. I looked down at my torn-up tennis shoes, gaping holes in my jeans, my dirt-riddled hands, and the white tank top I'd been wearing for months and smelled the fresh scent of my body odor. I could see the mess of my dirty, crusty brown hair inching into the corners of my eyes. *Fuck Albert. For you, lady, I'm Justin.* So I opened my mouth to give her a simple 'yup,' but she started going off before I could breathe out a note.

"Justin, we've been watching you. We know your past, present, and future. However, we can offer you the opportunity for a far better life elsewhere if you wish. It is up to you to make this wish. It is up to you to make these wishes, but I—"

"Wishes?" I said, holding my hands in a 'hold up' motion. Hitting an invisible wall that did not exist. With so much instant doubt in my heart, "Are you my fucking fairy godmother or some shit?"

These days had been rough, but I could count on two hands the number of times someone yelled a ridiculous offer at me. In the end, they were all just making fun of me.

She seemed taken aback; maybe I was rude. Fuck, I shouldn't have interrupted her. She continued, "Justin. This is not some *fucking* joke."

Damn, those layered voices sounded weird, especially when it was a curse word.

"I'm giving you a proposition: You will have nine wishes. You can wish for anything you want. There are limitations. But with each wish, a finger will disappear. Do you wish to have these wishes?" She stared at me through very tinted sunglasses.

I realized no cars had passed, and the light was still green. The silence was too much, the air still and quiet. I could not hear any birds chirping or the usual highway noise. Who the fuck was this lady? She looked angelic but sounded demonic. A glint of gold came from her jacket sleeve. Fancy watch, wealthy lady, and freaky circumstances. Did I want wishes? What kind of crazy question was that? She started tapping her foot.

Fine, I thought, *I got nothing better to do*, "I'll wish for your damn wishes."

She stepped forward and continued until she stood right before me. I could smell the daybreak, the whiplash, and the cinnamon spice of regret. This lady was a mix of good and evil, but at least she wasn't ugly.

There wasn't much time for me to prepare for her quick, snake-like strike. She grabbed my left hand very forcefully, and a table appeared. I've seen one of those fold-outs at a picnic once or twice. It just fucking appeared on the street corner. Looking back up at her after the mysterious table materialized, she had a cleaver in her hand, and the glasses on her face were gone. She had black eyes. She had deep, empty black *fucking* eyes. And in an instant, she sliced off my left pinky.

I expected it to hurt. I had the scream of agony ready and formed on my tongue. I had my right hand back in a fist, ready to give her a sick uppercut. But when I looked down at my hand, my finger was gone and dissipated into thin air.

What the fuck. What the fuck. What the actual fuck. My brain kept repeating itself over and over. I moved my hand left and right, up and down, and the finger never returned. I touched the knuckle where it used to be attached. Nothing.

So taken aback, I didn't see her leave. The table disappeared like my finger, and I was suddenly standing on the same damn street corner listening to the cars go by like all the days before. It didn't happen—a daydream. I looked down again, and my pinky was gone. The nub left over was slightly purple, almost iridescent like her suit.

I racked my brain for what to do and what had just happened, and I remember she said I had nine wishes. Nine? Well, fuck it, I'd see if it worked.

So I was standing there, and I looked at this random stranger who looked like a washed-up surfer off the coast of California. He had bleached blonde hair and sunglasses. He was blasting some hippy music. He was driving a Jeep with a noticeable sun tan. He was eating a banana while lazily singing along—an evening snack. He looked up from his jam session at the red light, and I made my wish.

"I wish for a fucking peach," I said in a slight whisper and squeezed my eyes shut hard for just a second. In that second, I felt like a kid who had just blown out my birthday candles.

And I was suddenly walking up to this man in his car; time had frozen. Both his front windows were already rolled down, and I reached my hand inside the right side window, and I couldn't stop myself, I couldn't fucking stop.

Woah, woah, woah, I thought while having no control of my body.

My left index finger was soon inside his mouth, my whole body balancing on the passenger door, through the window, and I watched him bite down. His eyes locked ahead. Again, I expected the pain, a scream still sitting on my tongue, ready to burst, but it didn't hurt. I watched him swallow. What a fucking weird thing to watch your finger get bitten off and eaten by a stranger. However, I got pulled back by a force I still cannot name. I was back standing on my corner, and time started moving again. The man continued eating his banana, unaware that my finger might be on its way to being digested in his stomach. The light turned green, and he was gone.

Okay, well. What the actual fuck. I felt a sudden weight of something in my right hand. All my fingers were still present, wrapping around it. It couldn't be. No. What? It was a fucking peach.

Lady, I don't know who you are, but you changed my life. To you, I am Justin, and I always will be. But to the world, I am Albert. And Albert has some business to do.

CHAPTER TWO

o, I got my goddamn peach. And these wishes were genuine. Why was I expecting them not to be? Well, it's not like I could fucking trust anyone.

I was standing there with that peach in my hand, and I took a bite. It had to be real, right? And yes, it was.

The ripest and sweetest peach I had ever tasted. The juice was spilling out of the corners of my mouth. My tongue flailed around, trying to savor every last drop. I turned into an animal. I realized I hadn't had one since I was in New Jersey. That damn peach tree produced more than my brother and I could eat every summer. An odd memory of Tommy pushing me into the dirt and calling me a bitch came into my head. It wouldn't have been the first time he did that, but I think that time was because I told him I didn't want a peach. But now, getting a peach was worth losing a finger over.

I sighed, exhaled slowly, and looked up at the setting sun. The cars kept passing; everyone seemed focused on a mission. The chill of the night started approaching. I had to move. In the middle of December in New Mexico, staying out here would make me a human ice sculpture, now with the rare feature of missing fingers. Maybe I should look into a place to stay—I had eight wishes.

I felt some coins in my pocket and had a ten-dollar bill. *Fuck it, I could wish for a hotel room,* I thought.

But then again, why wouldn't I wish for a whole Victorian-style house—the one that she used to talk about all the time? God, were these wishes a curse or a blessing?

I hadn't considered her in years, yet she was so alive in my head. She smelled like mint all the time. She was trying to quit smoking cigarettes, and she told me gum helped. She was smart, too smart, and if she hadn't found out I was lying, we'd still be together. Love exists. I would be disappointed if I thought true love didn't exist. But it does, and I had it, and like everything else, I fucked it up. Anyway, her name was Gabby. She was probably studying film or history in London, as she always wanted to. I could make a wish for her.

Yup, these wishes were a curse, my past was coming back to me at excruciatingly fast rates, and I wanted to forget the fuck ups of Justin, but this opportunity had arisen, and I needed to take it.

So. Albert. Fucking Albert. What would you wish for?

With two fingers gone already, my mind was trying to figure out which finger would go next. I picked up a rock with my left hand, which now sported a new look: no pinky or index finger. I tossed the rock. God, this was awkward. There was no force—such a limp throw. I couldn't wish to be a famous baseball player like I always wanted to be.

A shiver went down my spine as the sun exited the scene, and I needed to find somewhere to sleep. Somewhere fucking warm. I dropped the rest of the peach on the corner, covering it in grimy sand. I had decided.

"I wish to be back in my house in New Jersey," I said confidently. I missed that house so much. I had an image of the giant fireplace in a blaze. I could make the fire by myself now. As far as I knew, the house went to some distant uncle when my dad passed. I'm sure he wouldn't mind a visit.

I wondered how this would work because I was in the butt-fuck of nowhere, New Mexico, with no car and no way to get to New Jersey. So it was weird getting teleported. But it was exactly like those movies I'd seen. I felt like I was in a tunnel, going at impossible speeds with colors swirling and moving all around me. However, what made this different than the movies was that I fucking lost a finger during the process. I saw my right hand float up. Colors were mixing and changing, and as quick as fire starting in a hay field, a chainsaw popped out of nowhere. My fingers went down, but one stayed up, and specifically, the chainsaw sawed off my right middle finger. Fuck. I liked that one.

Again, there was no pain, and the finger disappeared as fast as it had appeared. And all of a sudden, I was in my childhood home, staring at the grand fireplace where I used to thaw my hands out after playing out in the snow. I blinked a couple of times.

I felt like this wasn't real. It shouldn't be. In what world did I deserve to have this much power? There were so many choices to make; I felt like I had control, but I had no clue if it was true.

Was I going to lose all of my fucking fingers?

I yelled out, overwhelmed that I had finally become in control of my life in such a weird way. Yet, I was so glad this had happened.

However, I was not so glad about the gun that was swiftly pulled on me by the stranger in my childhood home, who I assumed was the new owner. Or it could be my long-lost uncle. But this felt different. The fight or flight came in a little too late. I fucked up.

Instantly, my hands went up. I'd had a couple of guns pointed at me, and hands up in the air was always a good first move. Show them you have nothing to hide.

My mind was racing on how I could convince this half-asleep but aware man in a state of panic that this guy, me, who was standing in his living room looking like absolute trash and missing three fingers, meant absolutely no harm. I heard some footsteps upstairs as the wood creaked.

Fuck, he has a family. I mentally sighed.

"Who are you?" barked a low but firm man's voice from the right, where he stood with the gun. I was frozen.

Was I Albert? Was I Justin? What was the best way to go about this?

"I said, who the FUCK are you?"

He waved the gun up and down. I could see it out of the corner of my eye. *Great. He thinks he's the big guy.* The shadow wasn't too large, but he was holding a gun, and it was small. So, I knew the type. I approached this softly.

"My name is Justin," I said. Might as well, right? I'm back

home, so I might as well be who I was. I hoped that it came across with enough force that he thought I was a sane human, not here to rob him or fuck his wife.

"Justin?"

The whole mood shifted. Within the darkness of this room, I felt his scared, panicked state lift and evaporate upon hearing my name. The room became lighter as he turned on the aged brown lamp on a table beside the couch.

"Are you seriously Justin Johnson?" he asked me, lowering his gun and taking a step towards me. The light was dim, but I could see the side of his face. He had a sharp jawline and a little trace of facial hair. Given the time of day, his hair was short and messy, but it looked like it should have been styled and slicked back.

Fuck, he knows me. God, I hate Justin Johnson. But fuck Albert too. I should have just said I was John fucking Adams.

"Yup, it's me. Justin Johnson. Sorry for barging in like this; I just wanted to see my old house," I said, lowering my hands and putting them in my pockets. *God, it must be like 11:00 at night here.*

He flicked on the light on the other side of the couch, closer to where I was, and I was standing face-to-face with Jeremi fucking Koppalich. My resident bully. In my residence.

Fucking kill me now.

"It's been a while," he said, placing one of his hands on the back of the couch and leaning into it casually. The other was still holding onto his little pistol, but slowly pointing towards the floor. He was going to act all cool and not like I borrowed a shit ton of money from him so many years back, and I, being me, forgot to pay him back a cent. I hoped he wouldn't remember it.

"It sure has been. How have you been?" I say, trying to cut and paste his cool, calm, casual smile onto my face while crossing my arms on my chest. The T-shirt I'd been wearing for the last six months had too many stains to count.

"Fuck off with the small talk," he said. So much for trying to have common courtesy. "Where did you run off to? Did you think I wouldn't remember? I am seriously in the process of trying to fucking find you. What a blessing it is that you showed up." He gestured like he was thanking God. "Sure saved me a lot of trouble."

He locked eyes with me again. His grin. His fucking wicked grin. This man was evil. Why was he living in my house? Was this some weirdly sick revenge? Did he know I would come back? Man, fuck Jeremi.

He cocked the gun and pointed it at me again.

"Whoa, whoa, whoa," I said, and my hands went up again as if I were some jack-in-the-box. "I can pay you back right now," I assured him. I looked up and saw my fingers. I mentally said goodbye to whichever one the devil lady chose.

He didn't look convinced. *Fuck, this is where I die. The most incredible fuck up of all.* Jeremi used to get into fights all the time. He beat some kid black and blue for cutting in front of him in the lunch line. We were seniors in high school. Maybe he had matured.

Nope. He stepped closer.

"Hah, good one, Swanson."

Swanson. I hadn't heard that one in a while. I used to do ballet; I was in *Swan Lake*. I only did it for a short time before baseball took over. Long story short, boys who do ballet and are friends with all the girls are prone to getting bullied. I enjoyed it, though—the ballet, I mean.

"I'm serious," I said, lowering my hands and placing them in front of me. I noticed the wrinkles on Jeremi's face. He was getting older. Shit. He had a family, and they were right upstairs. My mind wandered to what they would look like if they had the same wicked grin, but it wasn't like I would meet them.

"I know this is going to sound crazy," I said slowly. I still thought Jeremi was fucking stupid, but we'd see what he proclaimed now. "I'm going to make a wish for the money, and it's going to come true."

The gun arrived at my head this time; it was not going to work. I thought of different ways I could punch him in the balls so I could run away from this godforsaken hellhole I'd placed myself in.

He exhaled suddenly, as people do when they find something entertaining, yet it was not worthy of a full laugh.

"Swanson. This isn't some storybook. By the looks of it, you're probably on crack. Is that where my money went? Are you a crack addict now?" He smirked at me and jammed the gun a little harder into my head. *Fuck Jeremi. Fuck this. I'm going to do it.*

"I wish for three hundred thousand dollars," I stated while staring at the giant family portrait that he had hanging over the fireplace. It looked painted and expensive, and his family seemed strangely familiar. The gold frame around it had intricate little diamonds inlaid, seeming to shine in the dark. His eyes were a crazy blue in the portrait, but looking at him, I was convinced they are just red because all I could see was the reflection of flames from the hell within him.

Time froze, as it usually did. I saw out of the corner of my eyes that his face was contorted and in a state of confusion. *Sucker.*

My hands were already out and up, so the finger-disappearing trick should not be too complicated. Would this work with money? I'd seen enough shows and read enough books to know that sometimes genies refuse to supply monetary value to their so-called 'customers.' *Please, demonic lady, send me some grace.*

The gun went off.

That was such weird precision. My right thumb got shot off. Watching it happen, I was looking up at my hand and saw the bullet slicing through my thumb joint sideways. That shot should have been impossible; hell, it didn't even come from the gun that was against my head. I saw my thumb apart from my body for one second; the next, it was just air. But I mentally said farewell to my thumb and got ready to face the angry man-child who still thought he was entitled to take my ego.

"What the FUCK, Swanson!" he yelled at me, and jabbed the gun again against my temple. *Ouch.* I looked around; where was the money? And then I felt something hit me in the face. The money was raining down from the ceiling. Ones and fives were gushing out of the ceiling. I guessed I was in a real-life fucking movie.

Jeremi looked up, obviously baffled. Flabbergasted at the

amount of money that started pouring down, Jeremi lifted the gun from my temple.

"Candace!" he yelled out, "Candace! Come down here!"

And that was my opportunity to evacuate. Jeremi was still stupid enough to be easily entertained. I needed to leave. Get the fuck out of there. Leave forever. What a mistake it had been to come back. Money was hitting my face as I booked it to the back door.

Luckily, the time I spent there growing up meant I could still navigate it, even with a blindfold. I remembered when Tommy thought that would be funny. One dull summer day, he dared me to run from upstairs to outside the house. He bet his cookie from dessert. I didn't hit a single damn wall on my way out. Tommy was a dumbass who lost his cookie.

As my hand grabbed the doorknob awkwardly, I realized I was homeless yet again. I hoped Jeremi would be out of my hair forever. I turned the cold brass knob and found myself out in the New Jersey air. It smelled like fucking tar.

CHAPTER THREE

The driveway up to my house had changed. There were gates now and more extensive fencing—the significant, old, iron type with a sharp tip on top—a stark difference from the tiny little white fence that had lined the property back in my day. The sun was still gone, but I could feel the air start to change for the morning. I had to jump the gate since I doubted Mr. Money Man would press that button to free me.

My ballet days were over, but my legs hadn't taken much of a toll since I stopped. Girls used to be surprised when I took off my pants. Thunder thighs, tree trunks, pillar dude, and so on—I heard all the names that middle school bullies could drop. So, using the strength from those energy packs, I jumped and grabbed onto the top edge of the fence. I wrangled my body over and landed back on my two feet on the other side.

Fuck, I need a drink.

Alcohol consumption was something that I was not proud of. I used to tell people that living a clean, sober life was the best life, and if I even thinks about straying, the love from God would protect me. I learned this phrase from my mother; the first sip of whiskey was from my father. Did I think I could escape drinking in that house? What nonsense I used to talk about. Growing up changes you.

Even though my driveway had changed, I looked back, and the house had not. It was a reasonably large house. My dad worked many hours to supply his snobby wife with the best place he could find at the time, Saddle River. The streetlights revealed the cool gray stucco it was now painted with, in contrast to the warm cherry oak it used to be paneled with. I hated this place. Small towns were meant for small families. But as always, the gossip was too big for a place like this. My father's drinking started soon after we moved here. Tommy and I were still very young; we were both born in Arizona, but my mother complained about the summers, and boom. We ended up in New Jersey. I didn't remember much about moving, but somehow, we got to the house. I was nine when we moved, and Tommy was twelve. I remember the first taste of whiskey that I drank burned my throat. I was ten.

"He's old enough," my father slurred the sentence together while taking another sip from the cup. His hair was disheveled from a long day at work. He was melting into the red velvet couch in our living room, staring at the fireplace. It was his daily routine.

"He is most certainly not," my mother stated, reaching for the glass, but I could hear the hesitation in her voice. She came over to me and put her hands on my shoulders instead. They were small, slightly cold, but firm. I looked up at her to see her face turn a little red between the wrinkles, and her golden hair, tucked

behind her ear, fell across her face. We were all in the living room, where Jeremi was now drowning in money.

My father stood up and walked the two feet over to her. I could smell the aroma of my father's cologne mixed with the secret smoke of cigarettes. He was a walking lie of a human, bearing the presence of a fierce lion. He faced my mother, and her hands tightened a little around me.

"My goddamn son is old enough," he was still looking at her, but handed me the cup. I held it in my small, boyish hands, unsure what to do. I was in the middle of it, as I always was. The ice cube was giant in the cup, slightly clinking on the glass. Before anyone else could say anything, I took a quick sip. I remember hearing my mother gasp, and, instantly, a coughing fit erupted from me.

"That's my son," my father said proudly, even letting out a small chuckle. My mother got upset, let go of me, and ran into her room. My father swiftly took the cup from my hands, walked back over to the oversized couch with a smirk, and took a swig that emptied the cup. He cleared his throat, put his hand over his eyes, and sighed. My cough had finally subsided, and drinking was everything but what I was feeling.

"One day, you'll realize that I am a blessing," he said, his hand still over his eyes. "I'm a fucking blessing."

My father considered himself a blessing while my mother counted her blessings; I didn't know who I was blessed with. I used to look up to my father, and I felt things were better in Arizona. We went to the Grand Canyon once. I only remembered smiles and pictures getting taken. It was sunny, and not a cloud in the sky. My arm was constantly around my brother, Tommy, and I held hands with Mom and Dad. They would smile at each other and share small bursts of laughter. Damn. That was ages ago when the sun felt warm.

I need a whiskey. The thought was urgent and overpowering.

I started walking to Avondale, the local pub restaurant I used to go to fuck around with my buddies from high school. I honestly wondered if it would still be there, and also if they remembered me. I was fucked.

It was chilly outside, but I was no stranger to the cold. I knew the bar would be open, and I didn't have anywhere else to go since that wish had been a bust. The tar-like smell came from all over, as the road had just been paved. The trees were pretty bare, but there were green bushes and weeds to counteract the lack of color. I didn't even check the driveway where Gabby and I wrote our names in high school when the cement was still drying.

"It will be there forever!" she declared, a cigarette hanging loosely from her lips. "But me, I'm not going to be here forever."

She thought she was funny that day and offered a slight grin to me while squinting up at the sky. Her left hand absentmindedly flicked her lighter on and off. I remember being hurt but trying not to show it. She wasn't taking me with her. I was oblivious to the fact that she knew more about this shithole than I did. Getting out of here was the best move if you wanted to grow up. That was also before I fucked up. When Gabby and I still had a chance.

Yet, here I was, a grown fucking man walking the streets that brought me bad decisions and now brought back memories I had hoped to forget. Gabby loved Avondale. She was even a bartender there once. She was 17, but the town had a kind of trust that only suburbias can have. She worked for a summer but quit because she didn't like the attention she got from the old creeps around here. I wondered if she ever came back. What if she decided to work there again? I put my hand on the long, skinny metal door handle and opened it with a hand that had no thumb.

The outside of the place could've passed for a diner in the '50s. The chrome exterior was mirrored inside. It looked big and small at the same time. There wasn't a sign, just a red neon "A" hung above the door. Once inside, it was the same as I remembered. Except there were no guns on the walls. Instantly, I wondered what kind of tight ass owned the pub now. For some reason, the previous owner wanted the bar to have a "dangerous" theme. Once, he told me all the guns on the wall were loaded—a secret between him and me. I walked up to the chrome counter. The lighting was dim, just enough that I could still read the drink menu, but I didn't need to.

"Whiskey," I told the back of a person standing behind the dirty black counter.

There was another man who had his ass on a barstool and was leaning against the counter with his elbow in a position that allowed him to support his chin with his hand. Glasses. Book. Scholar. By the looks of it, he was around thirty, almost my age, and looked up at me from his book when he heard me speak.

Fuck off, I thought, *let me drink in peace.*

The bartender turned around, and we made eye contact. It wasn't Gabby—just a regular guy with long brown hair. I felt a weird twinge inside of me. Was I embarrassed? Why would I even miss her? Why do I even fucking care?

"You got any money?" the bartender asked me. Looking me up and down, he looked afterward at the guy sitting at the bar. They exchanged glances. I forgot that I still looked like shit, and my fingers were missing. Anyone who saw me would probably be alarmed, since people who looked like me were usually never allowed to set foot in this town, much less a place like this. Hell, I wasn't even wearing a jacket.

"Yeah, I got fucking money." I shoved my hands in my pockets. I was sure someone had given me a ten earlier, and that should, I hoped, cover the cost of some shitty whiskey. I found the crumpled ten-dollar bill and showed it to him between my left fingers. My hands looked weird.

My missing fingers must have astonished him. I should have expected it.

People around this town got weird when I broke my leg. I think I was around 13 years old, and one of my friends dared me to jump off a tall rock. Everyone was convinced that I would never walk again. Rumors were flying, and I remembered going to school one day, and the teacher asked to see me after class. She told me it was okay if I took another week to do my homework, and looked at me with such sadness in her eyes that I started to get mad at people who showed me sympathy. People offered me their prayers. I wasn't fucking dying. It was just a leg on a human body, and for fuck's sake, it was just broken. Didn't anyone know that broken things can be fixed? This guy was giving me that look. That look of 'Oh, I'm so sorry for you.' I stared at him.

"Did you want it in a cup...or a mug? Did...you want a straw?" he asked me, and his voice got gentler as he listed the options. I knew he could give less of a fuck. Thanks for the service, though, buddy.

"Cup is fine," I said, rolling my eyes. I gave him the ten and sat down next to the bookworm. I was just waiting for him to talk to me. People around here loved to hear new gossip, and this guy looked posh enough. I figured I'd take the bullet before it hit me.

"So, what happened?" He used his book to gesture at my hands.

"I don't want to talk about it." I turned my head so my glare could be directed at him now. I didn't want to tell him that some strange lady uprooted my life by telling me I could wish with my fingers. I didn't want to say to him that my fingers had been chopped off, bitten off, sawed off, and shot off. I didn't want to tell him I didn't know what to wish for. He wouldn't believe me, but he couldn't leave me alone.

He wore glasses that made his brown eyes seem like he was swimming in a fishbowl. The glasses looked unique and expensive, with a gold pattern on the sides. He took them off and set his book down. He gave a gentle nod and cleared his throat.

"If this guy wants any more drinks, they're on me," he piped to the bartender.

Great, I'm stuck here. But also, you don't know what you just did, sir.

I was handed the whiskey while still receiving one-sided eye contact from this dick who thought he was the new shit.

There I was, with my six fingers; I used to have ten. So hey, you're all caught up. Anyways. Welcome. My life is still a shithole.

I decided to investigate this new Avondale visually. Not many other people were in the pub. At one of the booths, a couple sat enveloped in their own world. There were young kids playing pool and money on the table—a worthy bet. I could've whipped their asses if I had all my fingers still. Doubt I'd be any good like this. I shot down the whiskey in one solid swig. I used my left hand to hold the cup, as my right was missing its thumb. Holding things would become much more difficult once I lost my other thumb. I gestured to the bartender, who was still staring at me, saying that I want another, and he got to work. I turned back to Mister Scholar Man.

"What?" I tried to make lasers shoot out of my eyes—daggers. I didn't want to know what this man had to say, but there was a part of me that says I did.

"I'm so sorry," he tried to be polite. "I would like to know what happened to you. I am a writer, and I am intrigued by interesting characters. You presented yourself, and I would love to know your story. Please, if you would, tell me what happened."

Prick.

He folded his hands under his chin like a little school kid. His eyes never locked with mine, but they were fixated on my hands and fingers, and he settled on the iridescent purple nub. He was a fucking snake. I wouldn't tell him shit.

"I jerked off too much and got an infection," I shrugged and turned away. Another glass of whiskey appeared before me, and just as fast as it was there, it went into my mouth and burned down my throat. I enjoyed the burn now; I hadn't coughed again since my first taste.

The man was unconvinced, and I could sense the frustration that started to steam off him.

"My name is Harley," he said, reaching out his hand. His perfect hand. What an asshole. He wanted to touch my hand to see if it was real. I felt like I already knew these tricks.

"I'm Albert," I told him, still looking at him, but I did not reach out my hand. I let him hold his out awkwardly for a bit longer. He finally looked at me; his eyes were dark brown and almost black. It looked like he had been crying; his face was splotchy red and puffy. His light brown hair was a mess on top of his head, but suggested that he once had a gelled, slick-back look. He was pretty built and ran in his free time. He swayed slightly forward, still waiting for my hand. Perhaps he was buzzed, drunk even. He eventually put his hand away, and I could tell he was still trying to read me like that book in front of him that was open on page three.

Slow reader, I thought, *or maybe he just got here. Too drunk to read, maybe? What if he was waiting for me?*

Paranoid. I knew this feeling. I didn't consider what made the demon lady say she knew my past, my present, and my future. Suddenly, I felt like I was being watched. Did she have spies watching me? Was I under surveillance now? I shouldn't share anything. *I'm a closed vault; this guy isn't cracking anything wide open.* So I made a bet I was sure he would lose.

“I’ll tell you my story if you can keep up with me.” I made a ‘cheers’ gesture with my glass.

The next thing I know, there were ten empty glasses in front of me, and Scholar Man and I were laughing about the color purple.

CHAPTER
FOUR

o if you can make these marvelous wishes, why don't you just wish for your fingers back?" Harley said it first, but I swear I had heard it before. His fancy glasses were resting on top of the book now. The words came out of a half-opened mouth as Harley had the side of his face resting on the bar counter. The alcohol had taken over his body. His arms were limp at his sides, and I wondered how his body was in that position and if he wasn't sliding onto the shiny hardwood floor.

I wondered how I was still sitting up. Not a cogent thought floated in my mind, so I laughed.

"You think I haven't thought of that?" I said, trying to sound smart like I always do. "Fuck, I could have wished for more fingers!"

"Shit!" Harley sat up really fast, "You're a genius!"

His eyes were glassy, his speech was simple, and his mouth had too much saliva. I knew he couldn't match the intake I was used to. I patted myself on the back for profiling this guy correctly. Hopefully, he'd forget all of this shit by tomorrow. I knew he didn't know how to handle his alcohol, and he for sure did not know how to handle what I was going to say next.

"Should I try it?" I asked him directly. The grip on my whiskey glass got a little tighter. Everyone had left the bar a while ago, and the bartender had gone to the back and hadn't returned in quite a while. But then again, I could have just been drunk. Harley had become an acquaintance for now.

He agreed to the stupid deal I made, and by the fourth shot, I was telling him about the disappearing table and cleaver. I told him about the beautiful lady; he seemed a little too interested in her, but I told him everything I knew. He asked me if she was wearing a watch, which I thought was fucking weird. I remembered the wink of gold from her wrist but decided not to tell him. He cringed when I told him about the stranger biting my finger off, but I shrugged it off as I had before. I thought to myself at one point, "Why am I saying all this?" and concluded that I hadn't had a friend I could talk to in many years. I'd been trying to hide, leaving no trace for so long. It felt good to be open. It felt nice to tell him that I didn't understand what the fuck was happening. But he was wasted; how much of this would he really remember?

"Alllrright," I said, hearing the slur in my voice as I tried to stand up. It had to be deep into the early morning. My feet felt heavy, and my body relied too much on them. Before I knew it, my kneecaps locked, my legs gave out, and I was well on my way to receiving a black eye from the corner of the bar counter, but someone caught me. I smelled mint.

"What the fuck are you doing here?"

The tone was not friendly. The grip on my shoulders was

from familiar, cold, sturdy hands. I felt my heart, along with my shirt, get tighter. My drunk mind could only think of one goddamn name.

"Gabby!" The name came out of me before I could stop it, and then she dropped me. Luckily, I felt my legs again, and I stood up straight and looked back into those green eyes. She was blurry at first but slowly started coming into focus.

Harley was surprised because I almost just fucking died, and this mysterious lady caught me. Wide-eyed and jaw poised open, he leaned on the counter slightly too much when he said, "Gaaaaabby!"

Saying her name repeatedly made her feel like a hero in this situation. It was as if her showing up had saved me and everything, and Harley and I should owe her our lives now. Our drunk asses knew that wasn't the case, however.

Gabby had a short auburn haircut that came about to her shoulders. She never could cut it short when she was in school. She always told me she hated it being long, and I knew it was because her mother never let her cut it while she was growing up, besides the occasional trim. Gabby displayed a constant state of rebellion. She wore a leather jacket that was paired with a light blue scarf. The rest of her was just dark. Black pants, black boots, black gloves, and black eyes. She was mad. I was drunk.

"Fancy meeting you here," I muttered, and lifted my empty cup to mock clinking glasses with her.

"Justin. I'm not dealing with your bullshit right now." Her face didn't move when she said this. Harley gasped.

"JUSTIN! You told me you were Albert!" He almost sounded hurt.

Well fuck it all, I thought, *everything sucks*.

I had the urge to leave. I wanted to run and never see this bar or these faces again. Harley had covered my tab anyway. So, I tried. I turned and put one foot in front of the other, and before I knew it, I was outside hearing voices calling "Albert" or "Justin," but I didn't want to reply. I didn't want to be here. So I just left and started to jog, which turned into running, so I ran aimlessly for ten minutes.

I was cold, so I sat down on the curb facing the street. No cars were out; it was still too early in the morning. I was still feeling a buzz and wanted to try something that I hadn't gotten a chance to do earlier.

I took a deep breath and tried not to slur as the words came out, "I wish for my fingers back."

It was oddly silent. A shiver went down my back, but it didn't seem like time had frozen like it usually did.

"Did you hear me!" I yelled, "I want my goddamn FINGERS back!"

Nothing. *What the fuck was this? Was this wish just impossible to make? Did I just get rejected? The silent treatment?*

I opened my mouth to try again, but I heard footsteps approaching behind me.

Fuck, please don't let it be Gabby.

"Didn't work, eh?" Harley said. His glasses looked tilted to the point where they could fall off his face at any moment, but they didn't. He plopped down beside me on this lonely street curb and let out a big breath. Relieved that it wasn't Gabby but still not wanting to talk to Harley, I did what any gentleman would do.

"Fuck off," I said.

"I don't think you meant that." His tone became oddly gentle, and he placed his hand on my shoulder. It was a weird move. I wondered if he was still buzzed.

"I was hoping that you could help me out," he continued, and again, he didn't meet my eyes. For him, my fingers were more attractive to look at. He started to reach into his coat pocket, and I began to lean away, unsure of what was going to happen.

"I've been watching you for a while now, Justin," he said, using Justin instead of Albert this time—spy alert. "Justin, I know you've had a rough time and all, and please believe me when I say that drinking with you was such a pleasure, but I must do something now that you won't like. Believe me, I need it more than you do."

I watched him slowly pull a knife out of his pocket. His hand was sliding down my arm, getting close to my hand. It was a long dagger, one of the wavy ones.

"You see, Justin—" I hated him saying my name; it sounded wrong— "I have a little, shall we say, quarrel with the lady who gave you these 'magical fingers,' and I was hoping to get back on her good side. I need to make it right. But, I do need a wish first."

He smiled at me. His hand was on top of mine now; he was hot, and mine was as cold as a frozen turkey. The knife he had fished out of his pocket glinted in the street lamp. It looked more like an ancient artifact than something he could purchase at the hunting shop.

Fucking hell, he's going to cut off one of my fingers. I thought. *Maybe he's going to cut my whole hand off.* All I knew was that, at this point, I couldn't care less about what happened. I just gave up.

He held my right pinky finger in his hand. I just wanted this to be over. I knew it wasn't going to hurt; I was either drunk enough, or the magic would take over, and the procedure would be certified painless. I forgot that this so-called 'Harley' was still talking.

"—so you see, I can never get it back. But you have allowed me to obtain it again! As we found out, these fingers should be able to wish for anything but more fingers. So, I will wish my wish, and Gabby will never fuck me over again."

This, I thought, *is some drunk shit.*

He raised the knife a little and placed my hand along with my finger, still being gripped tightly onto the cold pavement.

"I wish for the..." he started confidently. His accent had started coming out within the last five minutes. I couldn't make it out, but he was not from Jersey.

The next thing I knew, I felt his warm blood splatter on my face.

Chapter Five

hank God for Gabby.

With a swift gesture and the power of swinging a baseball bat for years, Gabby cleanly decapitated my good friend, Harley. I couldn't have been happier.

She held the ax at her side and looked down at me.

"The fuck is up with your fingers?" she asked me offhandedly. She knew it wouldn't be answered, but the thought was nice.

"Who the fuck was this guy?" I asked her in return, getting up from the now-murder scene.

"Ex-boyfriend," she said casually, "He took all my money and killed my cat."

I raised an eyebrow. Gabby and I knew each other. It was in the past, but I'm assuming that Gabby still had past Gabby traits. And I knew that was a fucking lie. But, all in all, I did know her, and making a joke like that meant that she didn't want to talk about it right now, if at all, so I shrugged it off.

"Come on," she said, wiping the ax blade on the side of her coat, leaving a gnarly but fashionable blood brush stroke. Her heavy boots started walking away from me.

I got up and waddled along. My head was pounding, and I could smell Harley's blood on me, but I knew that I could trust Gabby. I finally felt the cold and shivered while staying about a foot away from her.

We didn't talk at all on the walk to her house; in my head, I wanted to ask if her family still lived there, and if our cat that we had gotten would still be there, or maybe Harley did kill her cat, and Pickles did meet her eventual death. But I didn't. I let my brain go haywire on what her house contained. Her family was, as most families are, complicated. They never really liked me, but I knew that if they were home right now, this circumstance would not be what they were hoping for their daughter. Gabby had a younger brother who looked up to me while we were dating for a little while. I used to call him Duckie because he walked a little funny after a car accident when he was tiny. He liked the nickname, though, and she thought it was cute. I think Justin had a good run in this town. I had friends and a hot-ass girlfriend. I was good at baseball, and my future looked bright.

Still does look fucking bright, I thought; *gotta keep positive.*

We reached her front porch, and her house had changed completely. No tire swing was hanging off the giant oak in the front yard; that tree was now gone. It looked like the house was a dark brown now, the polar opposite of the yellow it used to be. It made me think that her mom had died since she had it painted yellow while Gabby was still in high school. Her mom was a nutcase; at least, that's what I always heard. She wanted it yellow 'so that you could feel the happy.' Whatever the fuck that meant. We made our way through the front door.

"No one is here; you can sleep on the couch," she said, gesturing to the giant dark brown couch I almost ran into. She walked into the kitchen and started turning on the lights. She placed the ax on its rightful hooks, and I noticed more hooks held more axes. And guns. And swords. Gabby was a fucking assassin. How did she get this wall of weapons? It reminded me of the wall from Avondale. Maybe she took all the guns from there. I hoped she wouldn't kill me. I was so far gone from all the alcohol I had consumed that I couldn't find the words to point out the wall of doom. I sat down on the couch and slowly melted into it, and my last thought was about how it smelled like my brother.

CHAPTER SIX

hen I woke up, I felt the headache before it started, but being a veteran of this whole "drunk" thing, I knew the consequences and also how to deal with them. My secret is to drink tomato soup. Like, just chug the fucking can, and that is the ultimate hangover cure I have found.

Knowing Gabby, she probably wouldn't have any tomato soup for me to inhale, so I figured I would go to the store. It's a five-minute walk from Gabby's, and we used to get our Friday night beer and chips there. I figured she wouldn't miss me while I was gone, so I stood up and walked out that grand new black door.

Once the sun hit my face, I realized that I had witnessed a man die last night. Should I even call him a friend? I knew he was bad news, but I didn't realize how bad. Judging by my past luck, he was probably pretty fucking bad. I stopped in my tracks.

I have fucking blood on me, I thought.

I looked down, and sure enough, I was a canvas of Gabby's ax swing. I debated using one of my wishes. I could wish for a sick-ass new suit, and maybe I could wish my headache were gone. I felt these wishes had value, but at the same time, they were worthless. What was I going to do with a suit? Wear it out for today, then decide it's not my style and probably give it away as the most likely conclusion. I could wish for my headache to disappear, but that was such a mind-numbingly small task. I could wish for tomato soup just like I had wished for that peach.

That goddamn peach was the reason I was there, covered in blood, dreading to talk to my ex-girlfriend, that definitely shouldn't have been so nice to me after I broke her heart. I could wish Gabby's memory could be erased.

A sly smile formed on my face. *Nah.*

I turned back and opened the door again. Walking in, I found myself facing the wall of weapons that Gabby was now the proud owner of. Every single weapon had a home on the wall and looked like it was polished pretty regularly. As much as this should've bothered me, I felt more at peace that Gabby could protect herself.

Her house was two stories, and she was probably sleeping the day away in her room. I strode into her kitchen, looking for something to wash my face, and I found an Easter-themed cloth hanging on the handle of her oven. It's November. Classic.

If I were being honest, I missed Gabby a lot. I thought about her when I shouldn't, and it was always so hard to go on dates or even try anything with anyone after her because she had this weird energy about her. We seemed to know each other on a level my buddies could only describe as 'mental.' I'd always tell them that it was apparent we were mentally on the same page, and they'd give me a half-hearted smile, knowing that my heart belonged to that girl. What was the most mentally taxing part about it was my fuck up.

I wet the cloth and began chipping away at the artwork on my face and body to create a sculpture of who I once was. The fabric was immediately stained red, but I continued to rinse, clean, and repeat. Gabby's brother's room was on the first floor, down the hallway, close to the back door. I thought it might be a good idea to check for a change of clothes, so I did. That hallway was long, still lined with family pictures and mementos , and the room was bare. I found an old track T-shirt and a pair of jeans that fit me if I used my shoestring as a belt. Fuck fashion.

Looking now somewhat decent, and still no sign of Gabby, I went through that door into the world to get my damn soup. I still had a change in my pocket because I didn't use it at the bar last night due to Harley's generosity. I really should've grabbed that guy's wallet off of him. I wondered if his body was still there.

I took a detour from the store pathway to find the curb where Harley drew his last breath. It didn't rain last night; although it was cold, no snow had formed out here. Looking ahead, I couldn't see anything on that curb. It looked spotless. Not a single splatter was visible, and I felt like my memory was playing tricks on me. I sat down in the same place I was last night and looked around. The sidewalk and pavement were clean, and there was no visible sign of what happened or what I thought had happened.

I could maybe wish Harley would come back.

Why would I fucking do that?

I could maybe wish for Tommy to come back.

Why would I fucking do that?

I felt the poke again of wishes I probably couldn't make. But it had worked for the money, and that was usually taboo. I stood up and walked to the store. Cold because I forgot a coat, I wrapped my arms around myself and blew hot air into my hands. Back in New Mexico, I got pretty good at withstanding the cold at night. I bought the soup, which was a regular human interaction between the counter girl and me. She seemed like she couldn't care less about my missing fingers and seemed more concerned about why I was buying a can of tomato soup. I noticed the little eyebrow raise as she scanned it, but she didn't say anything, thank God. Once I was out of the store, I chugged that can of soup and hoped that she was fucking watching from the window. People love to be nosy and see how mysteries end.

I walked back to Gabby's and threw the can out in some public trash can that was obviously overflowing. The stroll was pleasant; the sun was coming out, and the air was fresh. Not too many people were outside yet, just a few walking their dogs to go shit. Once I was back inside the dark place that was now Gabby's home, she was in the kitchen. I could hear the usual noises of breakfast being made. Unsure of what to say or how to greet her, I closed the door a little louder than I should and hoped she'd notice the unwelcome but welcomed visitor.

"Don't come near me with that tomato breath," she said, not even turning towards me.

Fair, I thought; *tomatoes are her least favorite food.*

I went to where she was and was met with the sudden smell of bacon.

"Thought I'd fix you up a real meal since you looked like you hadn't had one in a while," she said, now looking me up and down and realizing that I was wearing her brother's old clothes.

Her face seemed to soften.

"I found these," I said, and I thought of what to say next, but honestly, when it came to talking to Gabby, 'flustered' was hardly the word to describe the turmoil my body went through as I searched for the right words.

"I noticed."

She returned to cooking the bacon, and it looked like she was scrambling eggs. She reached for a whisk, and I made a double-take.

"What the fuck. Are you missing two fingers?" I asked. I stepped towards her. No way. The pinky on her right hand was missing, and the nub was an iridescent green. She was also missing her ring finger on that hand.

She ignored me and kept on cooking.

"Gabby," I said, taking another step towards her, "can you make wishes and have one of your fingers disappear oddly? Did an alien lady approach you? When did this happen? Did you know that that's also what happened to my fingers?"

I couldn't stop asking questions. I bombarded her for another minute with details about why hers was green and mine was purple. I held my hands next to hers to compare, trying to grab her wrist. She just kept cooking, but I noticed that she was missing four fingers on her left hand. She only had her thumb left. I pieced two and four together.

"Let me get this straight. You swung an axe with basically one hand, not to mention your fucking left hand is barely a fucking hand, and successfully decapitated someone?"

"Yeah," she wanted to answer that one, "I saved your ass."

A goddess of mystery, Gabby was. She hated people who thought they knew her and those who did know her—a girl after my own heart. I guess you could say I used to be a lot more caring. Gabby was the one with a heart of ice years ago, and I was glad things hadn't changed. At the same time, Gabby was a vault holding precious secrets that could help me figure out this whole 'make a fucking wish on a finger' deal.

"It happened to me yesterday. I still live here, as you can probably tell. Yes, my mom died," she stated, and made it sound like she was reading my mind, "but my life hasn't been bad. I studied history, but I didn't leave. I couldn't leave because...I thought I could still have a life with you. But you fucked Jasmine and moved to California, and then I didn't hear from you. Jesus, Justin, it's been fucking eight years, so let's leave us in the past. I haven't thought of you in a while, and then you had to go show up at that damn bar."

She looked up as she arranged everything evenly onto two plates for us. I felt bad. I fucked up. I hated thinking about it. I hated remembering telling her once she got back from the airport. I still thought she would go because I was no longer the reason she stayed, so I left, and I guess she stayed. She was hesitating. I think she was waiting for me to say something, so I opened my mouth, but all I got out was the start of an apology that never finished because Gabby kept monologuing.

"I don't want that. The 'I'm so sorry' or the 'I really fucked up' because you know you did, I know you did, but time moves on, and so we shall move on as well. Now, let's eat our breakfast while it's still hot and tell me about your wishes, and I'll tell you about mine. Then we have to go back out there because, believe it or not, Harley was not the only demon that was lurking around here."

So we sat at her kitchen table and talked about our wishes. A man in an iridescent green suit cut off her first finger. When the man approached her yesterday morning, she was standing in the pouring rain, waiting for the train after being fired from her teaching job upstate. Other men surrounded him, but they were all in very black suits; she said the black was so dark it was hard to look at. It reminded me of my stranger's eyes—the darkness where there should've been a soul. The man told her that she would get wishes and then proceeded to take out a cleaver; a table appeared out of nowhere and cut her pinky off. Astonished, she didn't know what to do but hopped on the train and went home.

"You know the first thing I wished for?" she asked me.

"Shit," I said, "world peace?"

She snorted. Her head turned towards the wall of weapons. Almost pointing with her chin.

"I wished for those," she stated, and was beaming proudly.

"Way better than my first wish," I said.

She turned and raised an eyebrow.

"What'd you wish for?"

"I wished for a fucking peach."

She lost it.

CHAPTER SEVEN

abby had also tried to wish for more wishes but was unsuccessful. She believed that you couldn't wish for more wishes because the stupid bastards don't want to give us that much power. Yet, they'll allow a wish for a wall of weapons and money.

She also tried to wish for her mom to return, but was unsuccessful. She also said that when she did it, she passed out afterward. Unsure if it was from the wish or her exhaustion, Gabby claimed it wasn't possible. She covered a lot of bases when she first found out she could wish.

Her conclusion was: Can't wish for the dead. Can't wish for more wishes. Can't wish for your fingers back. Can't wish for people to fall in love with you.

Apparently, she tried to make the waiter at the restaurant where she had dinner fall in love with her. It didn't work, and he wasn't interested.

"So," I started, "what's the plan now? Are we going to become this rootin' tootin' pair of fingerless assassins?"

No hesitation from her, "Yeah, if you want to."

I suppose I had nothing else to do with my time. She could use another person, perhaps with more fingers, to help her kill whatever the fuck was out there. I got up and looked at her axes, guns, and swords.

"Why swords?" I asked.

"Always thought they were cool, and yeah, I do know how to use one correctly," she said, matter-of-factly. She sat back in her chair and crossed her arms.

Well, that's fucking cool, I thought.

I picked up one of the swords. It was pure, smooth silver all over, but the handle had a mermaid engraving. It was small, like a dagger, and could fit in my pocket if I wanted it to. The arms of the mermaid were pointed up towards the blade, and her hands were almost holding it. The tail curved and wrapped around the hilt, fitting perfectly in my palm, its weird texture a welcome contrast. The light bounced off it as she seemed to wink at me.

"Is that your weapon of choice, Swanson?"

"Fuck you," I told her.

Gabby was there through all the Swanson stuff. She found the opportunity to bring it all up again. This cracked me open about how I got here, and I told her about Jeremi living in my old house, the encounter, and the whole money wish. She declared that we were going to pay him a visit. She said she felt something fishy about it. A Harley kind of fishy. But all in all, we were on the same page: fuck Jeremi.

The more the sword was in my hand, the more it seemed to conform to every angle of my hand. This, right here, was goddamn lovely.

"Fucking take it," Gabby said, "you need some way to protect yourself."

I was still unsure of what we were trying to protect ourselves from, but from the urgency in her voice, along with all the strange stuff I've witnessed these past shitty days, I'd believe if a raccoon started talking to me.

It was time to visit Jeremi. Our little talk would be cut short for now, but I'd learned more about Gabby these past few hours than I ever thought I would know. We made our way to the garage, my new mermaid sword in my left hand. Gabby had grabbed one of the axes off the wall, not the same one she used to decapitate Harley, but it was still sporting the same terrifyingly sharp look and even included a skull engraving on the handle.

Gabby told me that when she found out that she could make wishes, she wished for her dream car because, well, why the hell not?

The garage door opened, and I was standing face to face with a 1981 DeLorean DMC-12. It looked just like the one in the *Back to the Future* movies.

"Fuck."

It's the only thing I could manage. But I followed her, and we got in the car. The whole feeling was ominous; I felt a weird déjà vu, too. I looked down at my hands while Gabby started the vehicle and found a place to put her ax.

"So what's your next wish?" I asked Gabby whether she

thought that far ahead and whether I should.

"Dunno," she said, "I'll probably figure it out at the moment. As you can see," she lifted her hands off the wheel for me to see, "I don't have a lot of wishes left."

Four. She had four left. I had six. What the fuck. Was I wasting my time? Should I wish for my dream car? Why the fuck not? I deemed it useless. A car would do nothing but drain my already non-existent bank account. I could wish for a bank account full of money. I could sell the car, but perhaps my wishes have a plan, and a car was never on the table.

"What happened to Pickles?" I asked her, suddenly remembering what she had told me about Harley.

The car was well on its way to my old house; we were almost there, too, because everything in this town is a hop, skip, and a jump away.

"I told you, my ex-boyfriend killed my cat," she said without looking at me. Her eyes were fixed on the road ahead. The remaining fingers gripped the steering wheel.

"So, Harley, was your ex-boyfriend?"

"Harley," she let out a big sigh, "was a mistake."

She finally looked at me, "I'm sorry, too, because his meeting you was pretty much my fault. Harley was a boyfriend I had after you left. He was local, nice, and charming, but as you know, I know how to pick them."

She snorted at her own comment.

"When we broke up, and I met him, he was obsessed and wouldn't leave me alone. He was convinced it was written in the stars and all that other bullshit. We went on like five dates. The first one was okay, but he gradually became obsessive. After the fifth date, I told him off after he took something from me, and then he disappeared for six years. All I knew was where he worked. Unfortunately, he walked me home after the first date and knew where I lived. Sometimes, his work would send me fliers in the mail. They'd be for his work but from him. It made no sense. Yesterday was the first time I've seen him since. He showed up at my door about an hour after I got home and asked to come in, so I let him in."

She turned into my old driveway. There were no cars in the driveway. I assumed Jeremi was at work—it was a Monday, after all. But also, with Jeremi's newfound fortune, he could have escaped to Italy.

"Harley came into my house and told me that he needed me. I assumed that it was one of those 'how to win back your ex' kind of deals, but his voice had such a fucking urgency. He'd changed. It was like I was looking at a monster. He wouldn't leave me alone once he noticed my fingers were missing; he became bloodthirsty for information. He even asked about you, which I thought was so weird. That's when Pickles walked in."

I didn't like where this story was heading.

She turned off the car and turned towards me; I could see the fire in her eyes. They also got dark at the same time. She sounded scared but delighted to tell me the rest.

"Harley wouldn't listen to me, and I kept telling him to leave the house. He was making up this nonsense about how he needed a wish, he needed to wish for something specific, and it just sounded like he was trying to cast a fucking spell. And I guess, in a way, he did. Something about time and a watch: he said some weird shit and gestured at Pickles. She blew up. Into feathers."

Her face was contorted. I could see the hurt, the misunderstanding, and the wrongdoing Harley had done.

"What the fuck," I said.

"Right? So, Harley is either one of us or maybe he's fucking around with dark magic, but all I know is that he is bad news. I didn't see a finger disappear. I'm sure there are others like him. For some reason, which I'm still trying to figure out, they want our fingers, our wishes. But what I know now is that what is happening is not normal. Justin, this is serious, and we must do what we can to protect ourselves. Harley could have fucking killed you for all I know. We have to see if Jeremi is the same way that Harley was."

She's getting paranoid, I thought.

"Why are we checking on Jeremi, though? He seemed fine when I ran into him. I mean, he was fucking pissed off, but who wouldn't be?" I pointed at myself with my only index finger, "It's me."

She rolled her eyes, acknowledging my comment, and let out another weight-relieving sigh.

"He works at the same place that Harley worked."

"So? That's suspicious enough to conclude that he is just like Harley and wants our fingers?" I gave her a bit of a side-eye but continued poking through her logic. "Oh, and also wants to kill us, maybe? Because he works at some place?"

"Justin." She got really serious. She turned off the car and put a hand on the door handle, but hovered over it. "They worked for Lent Karpel and his properties."

Fuck. Shit.

Lent. Lent was Jeremi's uncle, and throughout growing up, we heard stories of the great multi-millionaire uncle who paraded around like a king. From humble beginnings, everything he did was for his family and for improving the world.

After failed business after failed business, he finally found his passion in real estate. He started buying all the property surrounding Saddle Road, and we thought nothing of it. He was rich, and he was buying shit. It turns out he had a money-laundering scheme, dug tunnels all around the town, and got busted by Jeremi.

He was sent to jail for around 20 years, I believe. After that, I moved, but Gabby enlightened me that Jeremi had taken over the company and made the company go into overdrive and caused the town to shut down for two days due to a power outage. Why does a real estate company need so much electricity? No one was sure what Jeremi was doing with the company, but no one wanted to speak up. I got mad. If Jeremi owned this company and he was seeing an influx in money, why would he still want my money? Well, it was his money first, but was he just that greedy? I wouldn't put it past him.

"I think they're using the tunnels—those hidden underground passages—to trade or hide something dangerous. Harley was always so secretive about them, and if Jeremi's involved, I doubt we'll find him at the store anytime soon."

She popped open the car door.

"Are we doing this?" She looked at me, then at the house, and back at me.

"Well fuck it, do I have a choice?"

"Nope."

I popped open my door, and Gabby and I took steps to my old home. This would have been a dream under other circumstances. It was a massive flashback. Gabby and I had walked to my house every day for three years. I saw her face every day. I saw her in my home, in my clothes, and in my bed. Looking at her, some feelings tried to spark themselves. Internally, my thoughts were trying to make sense of my heart. While walking next to her, I tried to convince myself it was over. It has been over; judging from where we are now, Gabby and I will always be over.

Because I fucked up.

And I'm about to fuck up again.

CHAPTER
EIGHT

he door to my house was not dark oak like Gabby's. Jeremi had replaced the once-red door with one that looked like chainmail, as if the idiot were protecting the home from attackers—like us. How ironic. It matched the ugly gray of the rest of the house.

We stood at the door, exchanging a nervous glance. Gabby shifted her grip on the ax in her hand, and I could feel my hands around the mermaid's body start to sweat. This lady was a fish, very much surrounded by water.

We rang the doorbell, which sounded a simple tune, watched the door, and wondered what face would be behind it. The knob turned, and we were face to face with someone we could only assume was Jeremi's wife, Candace, I believe, the one he hollered at to come down once the money was spewing from the ceiling yesterday.

Gabby and I quickly shoved our weapons behind our backs and plastered on our best fake smiles.

"How can I help you?" Candace said. She seemed soft. She was one of those people who radiated a feeling of roundness and comfort. I could curl up into her lap and be on a fluffy cloud that would take me the fuck away from here. Her hair was long and dark, and she had piercing blue eyes. She was short, at least shorter than me. She also had a huge, prominent belly protruding from her figure. Of course, she was fucking pregnant. My mind cringed at the thought that Jeremi thought he was unique enough to reproduce and pass on his extremely non-unique asshole genes.

"Hello, misses..." Gabby started. She was waiting for a last name. What was Gabby's game plan? Jeremi's wife seemed unimpressed by our looks, and I knew we couldn't hold her attention much longer.

"Koppalich." Mrs. Jeremi's wife replied.

"Hello Mrs. Koppalich!" Gabby started over and sounded like she was going into the worst sales pitch of her life. "Is your husband home?"

Great, I thought, *Gabby was making this way too obvious.*

It took me a moment to realize that Mrs. Koppalich had no idea who we were, even though I had been in her house and had spoken with her husband. She was still staring at Gabby with uncertainty in her eyes, and I knew we'd lose her in a second, or at least with whatever the next thing Gabby says out of her mouth.

Fuck this, I'm stepping in.

"I believe we have an item your husband would be interested in, Mrs. Koppalich!"

A sly smile appeared, and she took a small step back.

"Thank you, but I don't think we're interested," she said, slowly inching the door shut.

I pulled the sword out behind my back, and I saw out of the

corner of my eye that Gabby's face had turned a little whiter, and her eyes had gotten big. I held it in a way that concealed my fingers, almost presenting it to her.

"We're with Clashing Blades United. I believe your husband and I discussed this item over the phone; it's a novelty and a unique find. If you will, it will be one-of-a-kind, and I thought I would bring it for him to look at." I flashed the biggest smile my dumbass face could make.

Was I convincing enough? Thank God for looking at magazines while a gun was pointed at my head in my old living room.

Mrs. Asshole looked at me and made a strange face. Her sly smile turned into a huge smile, and her teeth were pointed just enough that she started to look like a shark to me. She was bloodthirsty.

"Oh!" She said, "Just fantastic, I believe he's been waiting for you! You must be John. I've listened to the voicemails, and we have a plan for our basement! Come in, come in!"

Gabby and I shared a smile; she was still ghost white, and I couldn't decide if it was because she was terrified that I might give these people her sword, which she didn't seem to care about because she let me use it. But I was no mind reader, so I pushed the thought aside, and we followed Mrs. Koppalich inside. She wore a white dress that flowed around her when she walked, making her appear to be floating.

"This place is darling," Gabby offered, looking around. I knew she saw the differences; the new chandeliers, not there before, shone on us like strange spotlights, even though it was the middle of the day.

"Thank you. The people before us didn't know how to decorate it," she said, giggling as she glided towards the kitchen, which had a giant makeover and looked like kitchens you'd see in books about interior design for a mansion: bare, white, spotless. "It took a while, and it's still getting there, but I can't wait for the final product. We're going to have a housewarming party."

She smiled again with her shark teeth while making a little clapping motion. Everything was so pristine and clean that it felt like no one lived in this house. The floor was white marble, and I couldn't see a single hair or crumb. The air was stale, and I didn't remember feeling this lonely the last time I was here. Probably because Jeremi and his good friend, Mr. Gun-to-my-head, were there.

Gabby gave me a side eye while we were following Mrs. Koppalich around. That felt like a "now is the time" look.

"Anyway, if you would like to follow me down these steps, I would love your input on what could fit on this wall," she said. Her hands moved swiftly and fast as she fluttered them by all the cookbooks stacked neatly on a random shelf. She pressed one in, then pulled another, and it also looked like a fingerprint scanner was in the mix.

Damn, I thought, *we're in deep shit now.*

I gave Gabby another look to relieve my stress. The whole wall opened up. Gabby jumped back, obviously unaware that this was ever in the house. Within this motion, her hand grazed my left hand. I was tempted to hold her hand, but decided against that. We were on a mission—a 'kill Jeremi' mission, not a 'fall in love again' mission.

I had a memory recall as I realized Mrs. Koppabitch's books were where my father's alcohol used to be stored. He had a small bar in the kitchen in the same place. One Christmas Eve, when I was around 11, I remember going down the stairs to catch this so-called "Santa Claus," but I was met by a noise I didn't understand. Peeking through the door that connected the living room to the kitchen, I saw my father drunkenly knocking a glass over. I heard girlish giggling, not my mother's.

"Oops," I heard him say, "I'm a clumsy fucker."

"I hope not," I heard the stranger answer him. They both burst into laughter, and something that sounded like a hinge began to move. I blinked, and they were gone.

With this in mind, I was curious now to see what this secret room was. She said the past owners didn't know how to decorate, so I wondered how she dressed up my father's sex dungeon.

Immediately, it felt familiar. I'd seen these walls before. We were face-to-face with a secret weapon room.

Chapter Nine

kay, breathe, I thought, staring at the guns on top of guns. One wall looked like the copy-and-paste version of the wall in Avondale. All very similar to Gabby's, too. Was I the only one without a weapon inventory now?

Even Gabby seemed taken aback. She was probably comparing this wall to her wall. Fuck, this wall made hers look like a joke.

"So Jeremi and I thought we could deck this wall out with more swords than guns. You know," she gestured towards her rounding belly, "kids."

Both of us were trying to figure out how swords were better for kids than fucking guns, but whatever, we're stuck in her messed-up world for now.

"Lovely," I said, trying to keep my salesman's attitude. I felt my face twitch a little. Also, I realized this lady just let someone decked out in leather and a man wearing ill-fitting clothes into her house. For fuck's sake, I have a shoelace keeping my pants up. Either she was plain dumb or this was a trap. "Where is your husband anyway?"

"Oh, he's upstairs. I'll call him to come down." Her mouth curled into a sly smile where her lips disappeared, and then she let out a laugh that made it seem she had forgotten that he existed.

Panic. Gabby and I exchanged glances.

"Oh, no, you don't have to do that," Gabby said, trying to smile. She looked weird, trying to be nice. "You're the lady of the house, and you know how you want it decorated, so please, keep going."

The missus smiled bigger, showing off her oddly pointed shark teeth again. Gabby must have been convincing, because she waved at us to keep following her into this dungeon. Once the door closed behind us, the chamber was lit with light bulbs that mimicked candles hanging on the walls. A giant chandelier in the center of the room had the same faux candles lighting it up, but also seemed electrified by lightning. It made me think of the small balls of lightning we used to have as toys when we were kids.

Crazy dipshit, I thought; of *course, he had to have those.*

Gabby was getting antsy, I could tell. Her eyes started darting around ever since Jeremi was mentioned.

As Mrs. Koppalich enlightened us with the chamber, Gabby did her best to agree and nod while offering some, 'Well, maybe this ax could fit here,' or, 'You're right! The guns would look better over here!' But every time, she would give me a look. How would we get out?

Eventually, we got to the part of the room that had taxidermied animals. A whole wall of them. Except something was odd. I saw human hands grafted upon pieces of wood, as you would see animal heads mounted. These hands grasped the air as if trying to reach their lives again. All the pinkies were different in color, shape, and size. Each hand had some fingers cut off. Fucking hell, this is not the place we should be.

I gave Gabby a tremendous wide-eyed stare that said screamed *we are fucked.*

She noticed but didn't care.

"And what about all these lovely items?" Gabby said, motioning to the crowd of wrists pinned on the wall.

"Oh, those?" It was Jeremi's voice. It came from behind us. He must've snuck up on us, and I wondered how long the bastard had been following us. He had a grin that matched his wife's, devilish in a way and almost charming. "Those are...collectibles," he winked when he said it.

Great. He was going to hunt us, and we were trying to chase him. I thought. I felt like I was rolling my eyes, but I hoped I didn't.

"So, you little shits," he said, glaring at me, "what the *fuck* are you doing in my house now?" He crossed his arms. The fake candles cast a shadow over him, making him look larger. He seemed so different from the last time I saw him when I left this town. Freshly 18, I cried at the bus stop because I had no money and nowhere to go. I was finally accepted to the same college in California that Jasmine would attend. My father had shut down any help he would give me since I hadn't gotten any form of a scholarship. He had kicked me out on the same day, and I hadn't expected it. Jeremi found me crying. He gave me an offer for some money. I was supposed to invest it in myself and my education. In return, he said he'd give me a job straight out of college. I took it—silly me.

The youthful spark in his eyes was gone. When he helped me, he was starting to work with his uncle. Still pretty laid back, he finally came out of his bully phase. He got accepted to a local college and was excited about it while he interned with his uncle over the summer. He reminded me of the surfers I would meet in California. That man was far gone now. His hair was short and gelled back this time, allowing me to see the full wrinkles on his forehead and around his eyes. He had probably lost 60 pounds. Looking at him now, in a suit that probably cost more money than I have ever had, he meant business. This was a business that this half-assed salesman did not want anything to do with.

Jeremi's wife was taken aback. "They're the United Blades or whatever people; they wanted to show you more sword collectibles." She motioned for me to show Jeremi my sword and for Gabby to show her ax. We were stuck between them.

"Oh, dear," he said, sounding very annoyed and hanging his head, "These people are armed with *weapons*, and you let them *in?* Are you the dumbest woman on Earth? You're pregnant, for God's sake!" His head snapped toward her, and he pointed at his wife. She flinched a little.

Not good, not good, we need to get out. I was trying to send this message telepathically to Gabby before anything got too out of hand. But she was trying to assess the situation herself. I thought she was trying to make battle plans on this miniature battlefield where we have enclosed ourselves. I was bracing myself for blood to be spilled or splattered.

"So," Jeremi continued, "You found yourself back here at this *great* time."

He walked towards a wall with spiked flails, chain nunchucks, and other sharp objects. Jeremi's wife, Candace, slowly stepped towards the door. They were doing a weird circling-us dance.

"This *great* time," he repeated, "my lovely wife has finally shown her true colors to me, and now this?" he laughed. It was gross and almost sounded like he was choking. He picked up one of the sets of nunchucks and spun one around while holding the other.

"All of this?" he put his arms out and motioned towards the whole house and the weapons. "For this?" he motioned to us all staring at him. Gabby and I were furiously looking back and forth between Candace and Jeremi, on alert for who would throw the first punch.

"I put my life on the line. Shit, I put my family on the line to provide a good space for the future that I had envisioned, and my wife fucking goes behind my back and—" He hit the wall with an odd amount of precision and knocked off one of the bales. It fell on the floor with a thunk. "And she does this." He pointed to her growing belly with the free hand, not holding the nunchucks. He was starting to sound like my father.

"I did it for us both," Candace started to say.

"Fuck you!" Jeremi replied and walked over to his wife, "All of *my* hard work for you to do a selfish thing like that. You know what, Candace? I'm kind of over your shit. And all of this. I don't need you!" He plucked another pair of nunchucks off the wall. The chain that connected them had some gnarly-looking spikes attached. He started to swing the nunchucks in her direction, but it was swiftly met with Gabby's skull-adorned ax.

"What the *fuck,* Jeremi?" Gabby yelled at him. Dude just tried to kill his wife, and she put herself between them. Memories and flashbacks of him beating me up in high school started to shine through. Damn, she's got more balls than I do.

"Stay out of this!" he screamed at the top of his lungs. "I'll kill you too! I *need* those wishes!" He seemed crazed and possessed. His eyes seem to start to get that red that they did when he was holding that gun to my head. In fact, his whole face was getting very red.

He swung again, this time aiming for Gabby's head. She caught it again, skillfully with her ax that almost seemed to be attached to her body. He erupted in anger once his weapon was caught in the crossfire again.

"She made a *wish*! You don't understand!" He yelled, glaring at Candace in between his clashes. He started sounding like a small child in a temper tantrum.

With a steady flow of tears falling down her face, Candace started to walk over to the other side of the room, away from the door, and as far away from Jeremi as she could. However, the wall she was walking towards was filled with shotguns. They looked like hunting guns, the ones with the long nose and big shells. I didn't know too much about guns, just that those were the ones that blew shit up. They were next to the wall of taxidermized hands. The correlation was eerie.

Yeah, those are for hunting us, I thought.

Distracted by my thoughts and observations, I finally realized that I, too, had a weapon in my hand and could help Gabby. I just had to figure out how this fucking thing works. Do I swing or block?

BANG

The explosion erupted near me before I could even figure out my footing. Candace, in her petite frame, had a colossal shark grin on her face again. Her hands were wrapped around a massive shotgun pointed straight at her husband. Astonished, Gabby had somehow dropped her weapon and ducked away from the bullets; her fast instincts probably saved her life. Jeremi, however, was less fortunate. His whole face got fucking blown off. It felt like time froze.

Shaking, Candace started to laugh, but she wasn't putting the gun down.

"Does he really think that all of *this* was *his* work? He dared to think that all of *THIS* was because of *HIM?"* She laughed harder. Her grin was uncontrollable now; she was going full-blown psycho.

"And you," she pointed the gun at Gabby and then swiftly to me, we both put our hands up instinctually, "really think that a stupid magazine title would distract me from the real reason you're here?" She inhaled deeply. "I can smell the blood..."

Her eyes turned red—all red. The long hair that was flowing when she walked started floating up towards the ceiling. She looked less human, and I couldn't figure out what she was. The closest my mind could think of was the lady who gave me these cursed fingers. Was it her?

We are stuck in a room full of weapons with a dead man and a demon lady, I thought, almost laughing at myself because this was my reality.

"I was the one who killed them all; I was the one who made all of *this* happen! It was me! I'm the one who found them *first*!" she declared in a voice no longer hers. It was deep and rumbling, almost like thunder. I was 99% sure that our dear friend Candace here was from hell, a demon summoned by dark wishes. Missing fingers, a room full of weapons...yeah, demonic origins make sense. Still holding the gun, with that awful grin on her face, she continued, "I only wanted to make one single fucking wish, and all I got was 'no, not yet' or 'now is not the time, honey,' but it was the time! I was ready!"

Finally, it clicked. She had wished for the baby. I wonder why Jeremi wasn't about that. Probably because she wasn't even human. She started walking towards Gabby, who had moved and was crouching around a display table of grenades less than ten feet from this monster. Suddenly, she stopped.

"He kept saying that it wasn't his! But I swear it was! Isn't that how this works?" She motioned for Gabby to say something.

Gabby seemed to be doing her best to stay calm despite everything that had happened in the last few minutes, and she tried to answer carefully to avoid escalating the situation. Putting her hands palm up, she raised her mismatched hands in a gesture to calm Candace down.

"I have never known of anyone who would wish for a baby," she said, "but I would assume that—" her voice faltered as she looked at the side of Jeremi's face— "wishes can be tricky. You can wish for something, but the outcome depends on the rules of the wish, which I'm still trying to—"

"It doesn't matter!" the mother-monster cried out, frustrated with Gabby's answer. "Now it's just the baby and me with all of our wishes! Now, on to the main course." She lifted the gun again and pointed it at me. I was just the dumbass standing in the same place, about a foot away from Gabby.

"I see you have kept a lot of wishes to yourself, sir. Don't mind if I do." She aimed and had her finger on the trigger. I put up my sword as a makeshift shield, hoping that it would block some of the bullets, bracing for an impact that never came. When I opened my eyes, Candace was gone. She was reduced to a pile of yellow rubber ducks.

"What the *fuck*."

Gabby lifted one of her hands into my line of sight. Her middle finger on her right hand was missing. She had used another wish.

"You can't wish for someone to die, but you can wish to turn them into something," she said, half-smiling.

I wanted to punch and kiss her at the same time. Why didn't she do that sooner? Why didn't I? What the fuck?

I looked around the room and took in what I could. There was a dead Jeremi, a pile of rubber ducks, and two misfits that should get the fuck out of here as fast as we could .

Gabby had other plans. She put down her ax and started looking around intently for something, up and down the walls, touching and moving things. She kicked the floorboards. I began to follow her around.

"What shit are you looking for? We killed Jeremi and his wife, kind of, and now we need to leave before anyone finds us!" I yelled, hoping that I could get Gabby out of this trance.

"I need to find it," she said eagerly, her eyes scanning every corner, "It has to be here!"

"What the fuck is it!?" I answered back, gazing at the hands on the wall, grasping for something. For a moment, I thought of Harley. The desperation he had towards getting one of my fingers. Maybe he would've taken them all. I thought about how all these hands on the wall were once attached to a body. Some were missing a finger or two, while others only had one or two left. All the pinkies were different colors. There was one plaque of hands high above any other. Both hands were mounted; one sported all five fingers still intact, while the other had four. Just the initial pinky was missing. It had a silver box with an inscription, but it was too damn high for me to read.

It suddenly dawned on me. Jeremi killed his uncle. There was never a clear explanation of how he died. One day, he was awaiting trial, and the next day, he was dead. He never made it to jail, and I had forgotten since the funeral was a private, closed-casket service, and people stopped talking about it after a week. No one really knew how his body was found or the cause of death, but he was dead. Not killed, just dead.

"Hey, Gabby!" I yelled again because I had not received a reply, and looking around, it seemed that Gabby had abandoned me. I still wanted to leave as soon as we could.

"Gabby!"

“What?” I heard a distant echo and followed it. There was a small door, almost like an air duct, on the floor, past the pile of rubber ducks. I ducked down and noticed Gabby’s boots were on the other end of the long, small tunnel. I crouched down into an army crawl and approached her shoes.

“What the fuck are we looking for?” I asked, and before I could finish, I was met with a bright blue glow. This room was glowing. Each wall was a solid blue color. Gabby was standing in the middle, staring up, so I looked up.

I was two inches away from kissing the bloody fingers of a hanging body.

Chapter
Ten

anging by his feet, this guy was nosediving toward the floor. He was neither dead nor alive; he was frozen in time. The blood seemed to come from a cut he had on his arm. It was jagged and looked fresh. A soft pink glow was also emanating all around him. In the middle of the blue and pink tint was a purple hue. This room felt like it had its own energy.

After the initial panic and a couple of "Fuck this" mutters, I turned to Gabby.

She was quiet and observing the room. Nothing was in it except this man. He was wearing a suit; it didn't seem to be damaged, except for the whole right sleeve being gone, exposing the cut on his forearm. His eyes were straining as if he were pleading with someone or trying to see something far away.

Fuck if I know. I just wanted to leave.

"He's missing his pinky on this side," Gabby said as she circled him. "It has a pink mark on it."

"Shit, he's one of us," I said under my breath. Goosebumps went up my arms as I realized we were probably next in line to be frozen like this guy.

"Gabby, we should leave," I said, turning towards her. It seemed she was still pacing around him, looking for something else. Her eyes rested on his golden wristwatch. Hidden under the left sleeve, the glint of gold gave it away. Goddamn it. What happened to leave no trace? Gabby clearly never did Boy Scouts.

"This is his uncle," Gabby said as she undid the clasp on the watch.

"I heard he was an asshole," I offered her in return. I kicked myself for not recognizing him from the past or all the news articles I had read. He looked the same as he did in the last newspaper I saw, like six years ago. He was getting hauled away by the cops, and the same dead look in his eyes was present.

"Asshole, yes, but also an amazing, corrupted businessman. Seems like he never got the chance to see what happens to a business when you can wish for anything."

She now had the watch in her pocket, and I wondered what the significance was. I thought about the gold I saw under the woman's sleeve who cut off my finger. It was fast, but maybe she had been wearing a watch like this one. Perhaps that was what Harley wanted to wish for since Gabby was looking for it. They both had the same desperation. Harley may have wanted to win Gabby back somehow. I felt my face get hot. Why couldn't she wish for the watch anyway?

"Can we go now?" I asked. Still unsure if everything that just went down was necessary. Fuck it. We needed to leave before the police came. Gabby nodded at me and then towards the crawl door. I looked back at the fucker as I started to crouch down.

"Holy shit, he moved," I told Gabby. Stopping her from walking past me, I made her turn around and look.

As if this guy was swimming through jello, his motions were delayed about five seconds, but he now had rage in his eyes.

"We need to go, NOW," Gabby said, grabbing my hand and dragging me back out through the small door, past the pile of rubber ducks, while I ogled at all the weapons still surrounding us. My sword was tucked into the back of my pants, and walking fast was hard, but we needed to leave.

Maybe if we were in a different situation and Gabby hadn't just stolen a man's watch off his almost dead body, I would consider this Gabby's first move on me. I wondered if she felt how sweaty my hands were or the calluses I had developed from pushing a damn shopping cart all day for the better half of eight years. Part of me wished I had the time to process this and maybe ask Gabby out again. Before I could give that a second thought, we came face to face with a kid.

Fuck. Jeremi's other non-wished-for kid.

"Where are my parents?" She asked us with a blank face. She was holding a stuffed animal that appeared to be a bat by its wing tip. She couldn't have been older than ten.

Gabby looked at me, baffled, as if we had forgotten that these evil people had more spawn.

"They just went out and will be back soon," she said, trying to walk past the kid, still dragging me along by my hand. It was general, and the kid could easily believe it.

"They always leave me here. Alone."

When she said the last word, I saw her little pointy teeth.

Oh great. Another fucking monster.

"Okay, is there someone you can call?" Gabby prompted her as she continued to take steps toward the door. I followed her lead as I didn't want to face another uncertain situation. I knew we had to get out.

"I said that I'm always here, ALONE MOMMY!" Her eyes turned red.

Shit. What is it with this family?

Before anything could happen, I stopped and turned to the brat.

"I wish you could be sitting outside New Mexico's best orphanage," I said, crossing my arms. I knew they would care for her because they sometimes cared for me if I couldn't find a place to sleep.

As before, time froze. It happened differently when Gabby made a wish. I didn't feel anything. But this time, I felt the brain mist come in. It felt like everything was underwater. The girl's face was slowly shrinking along with the rest of her body. My hands floated in front of me; despite having my arms crossed, they became straight. My right pinky finger was about as tall as the girl from the distance where I was standing. While her body was shrinking, so was my finger. Within a second, I watched the girl and my finger disappear like balloons being popped.

The time came back to us again, and we got the fuck out of there.

Gabby said nothing about me making the girl 'poof' out of here. Standing on the front porch, I looked at Gabby.

“Well,” I said, “I fucked up; we just made a whole family disappear.”

“So what,” she said and shrugged as she walked towards the car.

CHAPTER

ELEVEN

hen Gabby and I dated in high school, I remember one day when she did not want to squish the spider that was living in her car. She would beg me day after day for about a week to kill it. It was making spider webs; she could see it crawling around, but I kept telling her it wanted friendship. Maybe if she were nicer to it, it would repair the dent on her driver's side door. She'd laugh it off, and I felt like we had forgotten about it and had gone on with life. But this Gabby, who was shrugging off my sending a little girl to an orphanage, was not the real Gabby. Or at least not the Gabby I knew. Maybe her views on having kids had changed. But fuck it, time had passed, and who stays the same? But for this weird-ass new Gabby, I noted this.

"You know we had to do it," Gabby offered to the back of my head in the car. I wasn't looking at her. I was still trying to piece together all the shit that I saw. She continued, "You saw all those hands! He was getting way too powerful!"

"Yeah, but we didn't have to kill his whole fucking family," I muttered.

"Justin. When the fuck did you get soft?"

Oh, fuck she's serious. I thought.

"They were trying to kill *us,* dammit! We would have been next up on his hunting wall. We needed to end it, or else everyone just like us would fall to his cruel fucked up ways. We did what we needed to do, and now we can move on to the next step."

"Next step?" I asked. Turning to face her, I could see a fire in her eyes. She was ready.

"Yeah," She said. "This."

And she held up the watch.

"Is that what Harley was looking for?" I asked, feeling the weight of uncertainty about what the watch truly meant now.

"Probably," Gabby said, like she wasn't surprised. She seemed to be energized, holding the watch.

"Fuck," I said, coming to a realization, "Fuck, fuck, fuck."

"What?" Gabby finally looked at me, not at the watch.

"That's how he did it. That's how he blew up Pickles. Harley had to have had a hand of his own that he hunted and kept. You can't kill it, but you can turn it into something. Maybe it was in his pocket when he went to see you...or maybe—" I didn't get to finish. Gabby stopped the car so abruptly that I was glad I had put on my seatbelt this time.

"Justin, you sonofabitch, that's a puzzle piece right there. We knew Jeremi's uncle was sketchy, and his business was as well, and if Harley worked for him, then maybe he knew about the weapons and hunting—"

"And he got his own grubby hands onto one of our types of hands," I finished for her. "But...he also wanted to wish for something to improve your relationship. He said something like it would 'fix' it?"

Gabby gave me a blank look as she started driving back home again, her silence hinting at secrets she wasn't ready to share. What I'd have given to peek into her guarded mind.

"Gabby, what the fuck did he mean by that?" I said.

As we pulled up to her house, she still said nothing. She was giving me the silent treatment, and I didn't know why since I had just given her a couple of 'puzzle pieces.'

"Justin, I can't tell you," she told me. She sighed deeply.

"Gabby, we just murdered a family together. I think you can tell me anything," I told her.

We both got out of the car and walked towards the garage door that led to the house. She was walking next to me, but quickly turned and grabbed the collar of my huge shirt. She was still shorter than me in her boots, but we were almost eye to eye. We were so close that I swore one more inch, and we'd be kissing.

"Justin, you have to believe me," her bright green eyes seemed to flash at me, "I can't tell you right now, but believe me, I want to."

"You seem to know much more than someone who just got these fingers yesterday," I smirked.

She opened the door, and as we stepped into her house again, she casually let slip that she'd had the fingers for eight years.

Chapter Twelve

I kept them all as long as I could," she said, her voice trembling slightly, revealing her hidden history with the fingers.

She looked at me, expecting questions, I guess, or maybe a response, but I just stood there feeling so betrayed. I was thinking that we were on the same level, totally clueless, but this bitch knew the whole definition of wishing fingers. Had she just been playing with me?

"Ever since then, I've been keeping low. Harley and I did date recently, but I never would have guessed that he would be a Finger Reaper."

"Back up," I said, bringing my hands up so it looked like I was miming a wall or whatever I could mime with five fingers, "Finger Reapers?"

I almost laughed too hard. This shit was ridiculous.

Gabby wasn't having any of it and got super serious.

"Justin. This is bigger than you think. These people, these reapers, are finding people like us who are innocently cursed and killing them. So that they can have wishes of their own. Jeremi is-well, was the ringleader. Finger Leader if you will."

I snorted.

"His uncle was the leader before that, and I guess I took it upon myself to start hunting them as they hunted us." She finished with another sigh.

She looked exhausted. The fire behind her eyes faded to that soft green, and she plopped herself down on the couch. Everything was quiet, and I felt like I knew nothing about the world anymore. If she had gotten these fingers eight years ago, that was precisely when I had left this hellhole. How the fuck did she not lose all her fingers in those eight years? I had too many questions pop up, and I had the overwhelming feeling that I couldn't trust Gabby right now as much as my brain and my dick wanted to.

"I'm going to get some air," I said as I opened the front door. Not waiting for a response, I stepped into a gush of cold wind. It was early evening. It was my second day back home, and I wanted to leave. I looked down at my hands.

I could fucking leave, I thought. *Gabby.*

This girl was a mystery, and I didn't think I could ever figure her out. She was and always would be in my eyes: a cigarette-smoking badass who couldn't keep herself from marking up wet cement. However, she was also gentle and sweet when you'd least expect it. Now she was different and new. Not the girl I replayed laughing, when I was sitting under the freeway trying to sleep. I had also just watched her kill someone. I guess she technically just turned the lady into a pile of ducks. She killed Harley, right? Assuming she'd been in this game for eight years, I didn't think her hands were clean. At all.

I kicked a rock and watched it bounce down into a drain-pipe.

Gone, just like me, I thought.

I started thinking about the timeline. When I had last seen her. After I had fucked up and cheated on Gabby. While she was gone looking at the college of her dreams, the last summer we were together, I panicked and borrowed money from Jeremi. Obviously, he was very interested in me and followed Jasmine to California. Too afraid of facing the fact that Gabby would leave me, I went first. I hopped around, did a couple of stupid cafe jobs, and worked as a mechanic, and then Jasmine decided she had enough of me and threw me out about four months after moving out there. I didn't want to go to college for baseball and didn't know what else I was interested in. School wasn't an option for me. Three years had passed, and I wandered around a bit, made some friends who got me into a construction job, and I was pretty happy for a couple of months of that last year.

Five years ago, I thought I saw Gabby walking down the sidewalk, though. Or at least now, I'm sure it was her. I could only go off her hair at the time, but now, seeing her with it all gone, it clicked. I had totally forgotten that we ran into each other in person. She was hurrying, almost running down the sidewalk, and hit my shoulder. I was sure I smelled the peppermint twist of gum rush past me. I was on a bender, the boys and I were out for a night buying beers and talking outside, but she hit me, and I turned to slur something along the lines of, 'Watch where you're going, bitch.' But when I turned, I saw her dark hair fly past me, and I heard something as she disappeared into the distance.

"I'm so sorry, Justin, " the lady said in a tone almost like a warning.

I never understood why she was in California, or even if that was Gabby. I was too blasted at the time. But now, seeing her again and hearing this, I was positive she was that girl.

After that night, my boss decided to fire me, and then I wasted so much time trying to find a new job that I eventually gave up. I lost my apartment. I lost my savings. I lost all the money Jeremi had given me. I lost hope. I met some people who allowed me to join their group for a while. Till they all busted out little baggies after a day or two. I woke up one morning to half of them dead. Then I was on the fucking streets and found myself in New Mexico. Gabby, what the fuck did you do?

I kept walking down the path from her house towards my old house. We had lived really close to each other, about a ten-minute walk. I looked around at all the trees and white rose bushes my mother had insisted we plant alongside the house.

"These will bloom and give the house such a welcoming look," I remember her saying. Her golden hair was constantly blowing in the wind. She was down in the dirt, gloves and all, yet still wearing a dress.

"Who the fuck is welcome here?" I remember my father laughing at her and walking away.

As I walked up to the gate, I could still see Jeremi's car in the driveway, which I thought was strange. I figured that the police would impound it or sell it. Or maybe the bodies hadn't been found yet? It had only been a few hours.

That's when I saw him—standing in the window. Holding the curtain in the living room, I know too well now. He had the curtain with one hand. His suit was pristine, and his face intact. He looked just like he did holding those nunchucks. The look on his face was no longer of a killer but of a joker. I froze in my tracks.

No, no, no, there's no fucking way. I saw your head get blown out by a shotgun, I thought.

He gave me a slight wave with just his fingers, and I hit the pavement, sprinting back to my murderess ex-girlfriend.

Chapter Thirteen

abby," I said breathlessly as I opened the front door.

I saw her move before I saw him. A flash of all black passed by me. Our lovely friend Jeremi had decided to follow me to her home. She was behind me fast while she held the door frame and kicked him in the chest at the same time. He hit the pavement with a satisfying thunk.

"WHAT THE FUCK DO YOU WANT?" Gabby screamed at him. She was standing over him now. He gasped for breath as he fell onto hard cement. I turned to look over Gabby's shoulder.

"Well," he choked out after getting some air returned to his pathetic lungs. "I was coming here to see how my old friends are doing." He gave a smile that instantly reminded me of his sharp-toothed wife. He propped himself up on his elbow and continued to gasp for air.

"Bullshit," I said.

"Do we really have to kill you again?" Gabby said. She was fueled with black fire and anger towards this bully of a person.

"You forgot, my sweet girl," Jeremi said, slowly getting up. He looked like he was going to pull something out of his jacket. Gabby and I both took fighting stances, ready for whatever he had. Jeremi was in a suit, slightly different from the one we had left him in, but I guess we both missed an incredible detail. Jeremi pulled out a golden watch. It looked identical to the one we pulled off his uncle.

"No way," Gabby said. Her fire wasn't there anymore. Her face turned a ghostly pale, and it looked like she needed to sit down or have a shot.

"Yes, my dear, yes," He coughed out. He seemed surprised that I didn't take a step back or react with the intensity Gabby did. But I didn't know what the fuck it was. Was it the golden watch to a poisonous chocolate factory?

"Justin," she said under her breath. "He can control time with that."

Woah. What kind of movie bullshit was this? To me, it looked like a simple watch. I was expecting a high-tech screen-glowing watch if it could do that.

"But how?" Gabby now turned towards Jeremi, "You have to press the button while wearing it to stop time and rewind it. I don't see how—"

"I had a feeling you guys would come," he cut her off and smirked. "So I set a *timer*."

What the hell, are we sharing watch tips now? I thought.

Gabby was baffled, though. Her mouth was open, and it didn't seem like her badass mode would kick in anytime soon. Seeing a perfect opportunity, I took it upon myself to make a wish.

This guy needs to leave, and since we are a couple of steps away from our helpful murder wall, making him disappear seems like the best option. Jeremi was still relishing the fact that he had the upper hand. I would have to do it now.

"I wish—" I started, but of course, was frozen in time. Jeremi had his hand on the watch and was looking at me.

"I like your new pet," He turned his head to Gabby, taking a few steps into her house. When he said 'pet,' an army of spit droplets took off from his lips. "Oh, Gabriella, why did you have to fall in love with *him?"* He gave me a disgusted look. One more step he took toward Gabby, one more step she took away from him. I wanted to make a move on him or at least return the look he just gave me, but I was still frozen.

"We could have had it all if you hadn't betrayed me four years ago," he told her and walked closer to her. She backed up opposite the weapon wall, and I felt scared. He'd corner her soon—one more step.

"Fuck you," was all she managed out of her mouth.

Jeremi let out a repulsive laugh. "Come on, babe, we can have it all again."

Babe? 'All again'? What the *fuck* was he talking about?

"Oh," Jeremi noticed her uneasiness. "You haven't told him?" He pointed at me with his hand, which wasn't holding the button I was captive to.

"Don't." That was all she said.

"Your sweet Gabriella and I had a lovely spur of a romance five years ago," he started walking towards me at the doorway instead. "She had been living with her mom and was supporting everyone. But she couldn't keep a job. She needed a place to stay, away from her mother," he winced and grinned wider at the same time.

"Poor Gabby. So, being my kind self, I offered her a place to live. My wife never saw it coming, and that was okay; I didn't like Candace anyway. Kind of a failed experiment," he laughed, "And the kid? Don't get me started on that weakling. I wanted to get rid of her earlier, but I'm sure Gabby would have said something." He was right before me now, "Thanks for taking care of *that*, by the way."

Asshole.

"When Gabby explained to me that she had her finger chopped off by a random person in a suit, I was intrigued; how could I not be? My uncle used to tell me ridiculous stories about figures who would come to grant wishes. Little did I know that my uncle was among the main people spreading the good news. But I didn't know that at the time. So, Gabby and I seemed the perfect pair to figure it out. I got her to make her first wish." He ended with a beaming smile. Gabby wouldn't look at Jeremi or me. She was shutting down.

Jeremi walked over to my face, close enough to feel his hot breath on my cheek.

"She wished for your life to fucking suck, Swanson." He told me excitedly in a whisper.

That was it—confirmation. It was her, and five years ago, when I ran into her, was the last time anything went my way. I couldn't believe it. Out of all the wishes you could make, that is what she chose.

"I made her do it, of course," He said, almost reading my mind, "You owed me so much damn money, Swanson, what you used it for, I still don't know. And Gabby was so pissed at you, it was perfect. Until you showed up here." He turned back to Gabby and walked around the couch, where he plopped his righteous ass down.

"Long story short, though, after Gabby and I took over my uncle's company, I froze him in time with his own watch since he was the only other watch holder. Then, I was the one who used the cleaver. Gabby must've forgotten that I had a watch," he laughed a bit, "Silly girl. After about a year of us hunting other Hand Bearers, she gave up the trade and started killing for the other side. She also told me she wanted to find you. I see now that she was successful in all of this." He looked around at me, at the wall of weapons, then back at Gabby, and then settled his eyes on me.

"I haven't heard from Harley in a while," Jeremi said. "It's only a matter of time before you turn into what we prepped for."

Gabby was so quiet, I didn't recognize her standing in the corner of the room. She was probably trying to figure out how to fucking feel. How to jump over the couch to grab an ax. I was trying to figure out how to fucking feel.

"Jeremi," Gabby's voice was distorted and layered. Jeremi was shocked because his head whipped around to look at Gabby. "Dance and die."

That was all she said, and he started glowing–that weird blue glow, just like the room his uncle was trapped in. He floated up off the couch, a face of pure terror frozen upon it. It felt different–almost like there was electricity in the room.

His hand was finally off the button, and I could move, but I didn't want to. This wasn't a wish that she was about to make. He was no longer in control of his body, as he began making motions as if he were dancing. One arm went up and did a half-assed robotic disco move. He was floating in the air, and it seemed he couldn't breathe anymore. His eyes were popping out of their sockets, straining to see that his life was coming to an end while doing the Macarena. I was unsure what to do because I did not want to hug Gabby or grab a weapon. This shit was crazy. After about thirty seconds, the glowing finally stopped, and Jeremi slumped into the couch.

I walked over to him.

"He's fucking dead." I declared, not feeling a pulse. "Gabby, what was that? You didn't wish for it, but he died. Gabby, he's dead, damn it." I tried not to sound so happy or upset because this whole situation was fucked, but at least the devil man was out of our lives for good. Should I laugh? Should I cry? Scream?

"Lovely," she said in the same distorted voice and looked up at me. Her hair was floating like there was static in the room. Her eyes were that dark black they get when she's mad, and she gave me a smile that only used half of her face. She looked weird and scary.

"I'll see you again, Justin." She said and then collapsed on the floor.

Then I recognized it—the voice. It was the same as the woman who had cut my first finger off.

Chapter Fourteen

Frozen, unmoving, I stood over Gabby. Unsure what my next steps were since she clearly wasn't here a second ago, and there was a dead man on her couch.

Think. Think. Think.

"There's no time for thinking," my mother said. A vivid memory of her packing a suitcase came to my mind. Clothes were scattered everywhere in my parents' room. I had never seen it this messy. She shoved handful after handful of clothes into the bag. "We have to leave now." Her voice was urgent, and I remember trying to grab her hand. The next thing I knew, my father opened the door with such force that the handle made a hole in the wall. He grabbed the back of my shirt and shoved me out.

God, I tried to forget those screams. I wished I could've done something more for her, my mom. I felt so useless. My father never gave her the space to try to get help; she never had a second alone. There was part of me that realized he must have had surveillance on her somehow. If only I had been more aware, perhaps

I could have taken one of those peeping eyes down. But right now, I could help Gabby. I could focus on that.

"Fuck." I tried to pick her off the floor. Not going to the gym was clearly evident in this mishap involving lifting her. I fell against the wall with her in my arms and hit my head pretty hard.

Suddenly, she was awake and punched me in the gut. She sprang to her feet and looked around like she didn't know where she was.

"What happened?" she said, her voice back to normal.

"You, uh—" I groaned because she punched me hard, and everything hurt. "You killed him."

"I killed him?" she exclaimed, looking at her empty hands. No fingers were missing that weren't there before. "How?"

I plopped myself on the couch next to our dead friend. I cradled my head in my hands. This was going to be a killer headache.

"It seemed to me that you got possessed and demanded that he die, and before I knew it, he was."

She looked at her fingers now. She counted them.

"But I didn't make a wish."

"Yeah, I didn't say you made a wish, dumb fuck; I said you demanded. It was like a command. He was glowing and in the air. What are you, a witch?" I tried to hide how scared and freaked out I was in attempting to confront her. How could she do that? Did she really find me to cut off *my* fingers?

She didn't laugh. But I wanted her to. She seemed somber and didn't know what else to say.

"This happened before."

“Gabby, you’ve *got* to stop hiding shit from me.” I put my hand over my eyes. “When?”

“When Harley came over. After he killed Pickles, I was so mad. So *mad.* And after he blew her up, I passed out. The next thing I knew, he was gone. But obviously, he wasn’t dead—yet.” She gave a snort-like laugh at the end of that sentence.

“Weird.” I sat up straight and looked at her. “Maybe you activate beast mode or something when you’re mad. Maybe these fingers are more powerful than I thought.” I looked down at mine. Only five left. Fuck.

I looked to the side at Jeremi’s appalling corpse.

“What are we going to do with him?” I stood up, expressionless.

“We have to make him disappear,” she declared.

Part of me was almost hoping that the statement she had just made would get rid of the damn thing, but it did not.

“I wish for Jeremi to turn into a pile of shit.” I ended my statement with a smirk.

I was waiting for it—the weird time slowing down and a finger getting bitten or chopped off—but nothing happened.

“I guess it only works on live people,” Gabby said.

“Yeah, you’re the one to fucking know that.” I sat back down on the couch.

“We can’t stay here,” Gabby said, looking around.

“Why?”

“That’s Jeremi, the leader of the Finger Reapers. He must have a gang of idiots following him closely, so I suggest we leave.”

I sighed. I was so tired of all this chaos that I just wanted a nap—or a drink—whatever came first.

"Here," she said, going up the stairs, "I think I have some of my ex-boyfriend's clothes that will fit you."

"I don't want Jeremi or Harley's clothes. Thanks, but no thanks," I said, cringing at the thought of wearing the clothes of some other dude I've seen dead.

"Stop being a baby." That was all she said as she disappeared.

She came back with a suit.

"Well, what the fuck," I said.

"Sorry, but it's your suit from prom, remember? You never came back to pick it up..."

I wanted to laugh and cry at the same time.

Why had she kept it? Why was I such an ass to her? Would it even fit me?

I grabbed it from her and didn't want to look at her. She just stood there.

"I'll get changed too."

I managed to get on the suit just fine; if anything, I had lost weight. The shoulders were still too big, and the pants were a little saggy, but they were fine. It was dark blue to match Gabby's dress at the time. I was going to rent it initially, but decided to buy it after my father convinced me I would need a suit for an interview soon. I remember having shoulder pads and wearing one of those lacey ties pirates would wear in the movies. It's embarrassing now, but Gabby loved it, and I was too stupid to notice.

I stood around for a while until Gabby came back down the stairs. She was wearing a baby blue dress. It was long and strapless, ending at her ankles. The prom dress she wore that night was not this one, but I liked the trade. It had small but noticeable sparkles around the seams, and she looked glowing. Her hair was pinned up, and her makeup was done a bit. She was beautiful.

"Wow," I said and put out my elbow for her to hold. "You ready for this fucking prom or what?"

We both laughed, and it was lovely. I couldn't really remember the prom I took her to. It was our senior year. Honestly, I was starting to talk to Jasmine at that point. I was probably too distracted and probably too drunk to really remember the night. It made me feel bad, but this seemed to be a small silver lining—a redo.

"Where to, miss?"

"Jeremi's house."

CHAPTER FIFTEEN

If I had known that my house would belong to Jeremi Koppalich, along with knowing my ex-girlfriend and I would kill him, I don't think I would've wished to come back to fucking Jersey.

We hopped into Gabby's fancy car again and drove the route we both knew by heart to go to his house. I did not ask Gabby why, which was probably my mistake. What else do you do when you're on the run with Gabby? In my head, I was debating whether she was some sort of demon like Candace. Jeremi said they were prepping her for something. Gabby didn't grow or anything, but she did indeed glow. And her eyes turned black. I started making a list in my head.

She looked over at me and smiled. Her eyes were bright, and her hair bounced along with the car as we hit a couple of dips in the messed-up road. She was and would always be my first love, and I never deserved her in the first place.

"Gabby, why do you keep lying to me?" I asked her. I couldn't stop the question before it came out.

She paused and stopped smiling to think.

"Should you really be asking that?" she countered. She was taking a stab at the lies that I told her before. I used to lie to her a lot since I was cheating, of course. I lied about where I was and what I was doing. Hell, I even lied to her one time about a concussion so I could spend the day with Jasmine. I was such an asshole to her. And that was for almost six months, and I'd only experienced it from Gabby for a day.

I remembered our first kiss, though. She might not think about it much anymore, but it was a memory I held dear. It was at my first baseball game, and we were sophomores in high school. I had just hit my first-ever home run in a game in front of the girl from math class that I couldn't stop thinking about. Once I made it past the home base, I was expecting my buddies to come and pat me on the back, but this crazy girl named Gabby ran from her seat in the bleachers and hopped a fence, tackled me in a huge hug, and we fell into the dirt.

"You did it!" she exclaimed, and her long, dark hair fell around my face.

That was it, I kissed her. It was sweaty, and it was in front of a huge crowd, but I didn't fucking care. All I saw was her, and all she saw was me. It was perfect, to be damn honest.

After a couple of minutes of silence and me reminiscing on fucking over my life, she finally offered something as we pulled up to my old house.

"I feel like I need to protect you, Justin. There is a lot about these—" she held up her fingers, whatever was left— "that you just don't understand yet."

"THEN FUCKING TELL ME," I yelled at her. I was over this. Something inside me had snapped. I was sick of fucking things up, and I wanted to know everything if I was going to be on her murder squad. I needed to know the details.

She was taken aback by my yelling, and I was too, but she seemed to get the message.

"Fine, Justin. Fine." She let out a long breath.

"Eight years ago, I was fired. I found myself at a bus stop. Waiting to get home, I was mindlessly scrolling on my phone. A man in a suit caught my attention from across the street and walked up to me. His appearance was dark and mysterious. There was still some daylight, so I wasn't too afraid. But once he removed his sunglasses, it was Jeremi's uncle, Lent. He told me about an opportunity where I could make a little cash and maybe even make something more of myself. It sounded nice because I had just been fired, so I told him yes. He was the one who cut off my finger."

Fuck, I thought with the image of him floating in that room. *How? How did he have the power?*

I held my questions back and waited to let her finish.

"After that, he hired me. I worked for his company, and he told me many secrets. He founded the Finger Reapers after coming across a mysterious watch that he was told was a family heirloom. I stayed with the business for four years. I didn't use a single wish. Instead, I was told to test items. Or hunt people down, almost like a stalker, and let Lent know where they were" She shrugged off that last part.

"Jeremi's uncle soon learned that the watch could stop time or freeze one person at a time with the press of a button as long as they were within ten feet of it, more or less. Along with this gadget, he also found a huge cleaver with glowing writing."

I didn't recall seeing any glowing writing on the giant knife that the demon lady pulled out for my finger, but fuck, it could've been there.

"With the two elements he obtained, Lent started going around and asking some people to participate in a trial involving both or just one of the items. He called it the 'wishing for more' medical trial. He knew it could grant the wishes, but wanted to test the limits. When just the watch was involved, people would freeze where they were as long as eye contact was made and you pressed the side button within twenty feet. A group of people could also be frozen, but only briefly, with a top button. This button was only revealed after Lent threw it against a wall in frustration. The top popped off, and there was this new button. Years later, when Jeremi joined, he learned about the timer thing. You could set it in advance, using both buttons, and the person wearing it could then be transported to the same place they were when they set it. I had never heard of it working as a way to avoid death." Her face twisted while she furrowed her brows. I imagine she remembered seeing Jeremi's face blown off, only for him to appear again. How clever.

"As far as we could tell, there was no lasting effect. However, whenever someone was cut with the knife, they would scream for days. The cut would turn black or dark red. It was as if the knife poisoned them with something they couldn't get out. Their eyes would also turn black and stay black. Jeremi would call this the demon state."

An image of her with the blackest eyes appeared in my head. It saddened me to think she could have been a part of the experiment. Shit. An image of Candace also appeared. Were they all part of some demon club now?

"When I told Jeremi about the wishes seven years ago, we had just run into each other at Avalon. He joined us and was obsessed with his wishes. It seemed like his uncle finally trusted him. They both wanted everyone to have them. Jeremi had told me that he had read somewhere, in a book of old Viking lore or something, I forget, that the cleaver would lead to a great event. Almost like a second coming of Christ, but in a way that could bring the world together," she sighed and said in an exhausted tone, "with the wishes."

She continued, "The lore stated that a cleaver housed a fallen angel, and wishes were granted to those in peril, at a price. It wasn't some classic nursery rhyme; it was something that I guess was passed down through Jeremi's family. His uncle was one of the first people to bring it up again. No one had heard of it in a very long time. Lent had found the watch randomly after a great-grandfather had passed or something. The cleaver appeared soon after. I guess the text on the cleaver led them to these myths. A couple of years before I joined, probably around the time we first started dating, Lent had his first success. After reading and researching, Lent decided this 'magic' would work if a sacrifice was taken from the body. Using the watch, they thought they could subdue the demon darkness from the cleaver. The first person with a pinky finger cut off and along with the watch stopping time, it was finally successful. He went wild. Because he lived, he started wishing for people to die, for world leaders to bend to his wishes of launching nukes, and apparently, he wished to have boobs. Out of all the wishes he made right after, only the boobs part came true."

We both snorted a bit—damn boobs.

"They killed off the guy. They had found a way to alter time and reality while changing people's lives. That's when 'Hand Bearers' and 'Finger Reapers' became a thing. The idea was that the Reapers could go and find a target, mostly hopeless people, down on their luck, and give them wishes. Sure, they make a couple of wishes, but once they're tracked down again, it's over."

She made a motion like a knife over her wrists.

"They cut off your hands and harvest the rest of your wishes."

I was learning way more than I ever wanted to know, but Gabby knew so much that it made me uneasy.

"Jeremi's uncle, Lent, went crazy with this idea and started grabbing anyone off the streets. He had made a couple of wishes on some hands that landed him enormous wealth. He started making tunnels around the city. He had access to everything and everyone. When he got caught, it was because Jeremi reported his uncle to the police. I think Jeremi wanted it all for himself. So, once they took Lent away to jail, which now I see was just Jeremi's basement, Jeremi took over the company."

She looked at me with a somber look.

"The position Lent offered me was to figure out these items, how they worked, and their limits. As for the watch, I found loop-holes in the time system: you could go back at most ten minutes by setting a timer only once within twenty-four hours. The watch could only pause time for up to an hour, for a group of people or just one. As for the cleaver, it only really works when used with the watch. The first finger must be cut by the cleaver while using the stop function on the watch, and it *has* to be the pinky, but after that, some spirit takes over, and that's why we can make wishes now. Otherwise, I did not notice any other effects. Besides, of course, going crazy like a demon."

She laughed at that. I did not think this was the best time to tell her that her hair glows when she's mad.

"Like Candace?" I asked.

"Just like Candace. The last I heard was that the cleaver, since it is a group of fallen angels, will transfer some of its curses upon you. I guess not all angels are the good kind. It's a sin, the curse. Essentially, passing on a bit of the demon. Most commonly, people glow, and their eyes turn black. But the effects are random. Most people end up dying."

"Okay, okay," I said, trying to shake the thought of a demon being inside Gabby without her knowledge. "That's all good and fine, but why the fuck did you date *him*? An asshole like Jeremi?"

She turned her head fast, so she was looking out her window.

"He promised me something when I told him about the wishes. It was a trade. He knew his uncle was up to something, but couldn't get all the information he wanted. One day, he caught me while I was leaving Lent's place. He promised to protect us—I mean me—from everything else. From myself. He also gave us a place to stay."

Did she know that she was a crazy magic bitch? Did she know that she had the power to demand someone's death?

"It was romantic, honestly. He believed in me," she said, pushing some hair out of her face. She turned to me again but remained looking down.

I wanted to barf yet again. I cannot picture my school bully being sweet to her. If anything, he was trying to get something out of her, and she was too oblivious to realize it. Probably focused on prepping her for whatever he was talking about before she killed him.

"Yeah, sure. Then what were the wishes you made? Be honest."

She looked down at her hands. Only bearing three fingers now, she wiggled the thumb she had left against the steering wheel.

"Well, you know about the car and weapon wall. The pinky was to wish. I just used my middle to turn the shark lady into ducks, and Jeremi told you that I wished for...your life to suck."

She wouldn't look at me. She wouldn't look up at me once. This has got to be bad.

"Then I wished for Duckie's acceptance to his top college, and I sent Duckie to school."

She turned to me after this. She had tears in her eyes, ready to fall, and I almost wanted to tell her to stop because she was wearing makeup for the first time in a long time, and I knew she hated it whenever it got messed up.

"I wished to find you."

I was shocked to my core. After all that I put Gabby through, she still tried to find me. The screaming and crying Gabby I had left on the sidewalk after our break-up was not this soft, crying, dress-wearing Gabby in front of me. Hearing her say that, I felt weird, almost like I was living two lives. The one where I was a shit boyfriend and the other where I was shitty but still loved. And the next thing I did was not any better.

"Stop," I told her. "You hate me."

She closed her eyes hard so the tears would fall while she shook her head back and forth.

"Justin, I love you."

This was too much. Too much for one day. I asked her to tell me what she knew, not to spill her secrets and then confess her love to me. Hell, she was going around dating my forsaken enemy, for Christ's sake. Still sitting in my old driveway, she turned off the car.

"Fuck off, Gabby," I muttered as I opened the car door and got out into the fresh air. I didn't even know why we were here.

Why couldn't I get away from this fucking house?

CHAPTER SIXTEEN

I heard her car door slam. She was out of the car. If I knew anything, that meant that she was not happy. Shit.

"Justin, you fucking asshole."

Those were the words I loved to hear.

"I just told you everything, finally stopped lying, and you tell me to fuck off? What the actual fuck?" she said, with an edge to her voice. She was beautiful in that dress; the tiny sparkles were shining in what was left of the sunset. This day had passed by fast. I was walking fast into the grass towards the other exit of the half-moon curved driveway, trying to get away from her. I don't even know what I was thinking tagging along on her crazy adventure.

"Gabby, what do you want? This is all your problem now," I yelled back at her. "I didn't want any of this!"

"But you do!" she yelled back at me. "That's why I gave them to you!"

I stopped in my tracks. Did she really say that? Was she the one who gave me these cursed fingers? She *knew*? Did she want me involved in her and Jeremi's silly little plan? What was the point?

"What the *fuck* did you just say?"

I let her walk up to me. She was still crying, and her makeup was running down her face.

"I gave you the wishes, Justin. I wished to find you so I could give you the wishes. I still had access to Jeremi's office, so I grabbed the watch and cleaver and wished for you, but I ended up in New Mexico. I found you, and now—" she wiped away a tear and looked at me with such trust and innocence— "you're here with me. Isn't that what you want? Isn't that the greatest wish?"

I could not believe what I was hearing. Of course, it was her. She had this all fucking planned out. I didn't understand why she wanted me back after all this time.

"But I've only been a dick to you basically for our entire relationship and friendship," I told her bluntly. If she didn't realize it, I was going to make her.

"But you said so yourself, you fucked up. I know you still love me; I see how you look at me." She reached for my hand with the two fingers left on her right hand.

I stepped away, dodging the soft touch of comfort. The fresh grass crushed under my feet. It was wet; the sprinklers must've just gone off.

"Gabby. No. At least we had a good two years, but after that, everything started crashing down around me. I didn't know what I was doing, especially after Tommy died..." I paused. I hadn't thought of Tommy since I first got these wishes. My older brother was a dick, just like I was. But he used to be nice until Mom left.

My parents were never good for each other. Just like fire and ice, the ice melts eventually. Unfortunately, my Mom was the ice in this situation.

She left us one lonely night in September when I had just started high school. In the middle of the night. She never contacted any of us again, just left the whole fucking world, it seemed. I remembered the night she was packing, but after Dad slammed the door in my face, he told us she had left the next day. Dad was elated and could bring over his girlfriends now that he had the freedom to do so. He would be drunk daily, and I honestly would try to keep to myself and not talk to him. He took out much of his anger on Tommy since he didn't attend college. After Mom left, he was devastated and stayed home, missing out on his full-ride architecture scholarship.

Dad was not too happy about that.

Tommy would do anything to upset him; he even went out to buy a motorcycle. I remember thinking it was so cool that my older brother was getting something both dangerous and fast. Little did we all know that it would be his last purchase. One night, after too much drinking, Dad got mad at him. From upstairs, I could hear him in his normal drunk state, screaming at Tommy in the driveway. Something about him having no future and his failure to us. In the middle of the night, I heard the motorcycle leave and rushed to see the taillights fading down the street. Tommy left and went off the grid. Dad told me he didn't want his family anymore. After that, my life started falling apart. During the years he was gone, I kept playing baseball to stay busy, but there was little joy in my life except when I met Gabby. Last I heard, Tommy was hit by a truck soon after I had moved to California. The truck driver didn't see him. I honestly think he didn't see the truck.

"Gabby, can we just stop this?" I looked at her with pleading eyes. I did not want to uproot all the crazy stuff from the past. "Can we just leave it behind us?"

"No," she said, but with this word came a slight warble of another voice that collided with hers.

Her hair was loose around her face, and a strand started to rise towards the sky. A demon state was coming.

"I think I want you to stay here. I wish for you to stay here with me."

She let out a scream that didn't sound like it hurt, but it hurt my ears. Since she had made the wish, I couldn't see how her finger was lost, but after I blinked, her left thumb was gone, and my feet were planted in the grass outside of my old house. I couldn't see the cement on the ground, but my feet were in it.

"Gabby fucking stop this."

"No, Justin. You stop this. I gave you this marvelous gift, hell, I even protected you so you could make all the wishes and look at you. Still sitting on four wishes. Pathetic. You should feel the fire in your blood. Why haven't you wished to go somewhere else? Maybe take me with you?"

She was circling my frozen body like a vulture. This voice was not her own. Her heels dug into the grass and dirt, but it didn't bother her. Chunks of grass flew up from her feet as she closed on me. She started looking a lot more devilish than I had ever seen her. Her hands were beginning to turn the same deep red as I had seen before, and the nails she had left on her right hand were growing longer. Finally, in one more blink, her eyes turned black.

I was stuck. So very fucking stuck. What the hell could I do?

"I wish to be back in New Mexico," I said through my gritted teeth. I needed to leave now.

Gabby screamed again. Another voice came out of her. She looked possessed. Was this what they were prepping her for? My right hand lifted in front of my face, and time slowed. A bird was swooping down. It was supposed to bite off my finger, and right when it had it in its mouth, I saw a glimmer of gold. I recognized the watch that Jeremi was wearing was broken. Gabby had shown it to me before we left his body.

My devil ex-girlfriend was holding a magic watch. I was frozen again, and the bird was frozen in mid-flight.

"I intentionally left this on his uncle; I knew it would come in handy," she winked. "Justin, I am *very* disappointed in you," she said with a layered voice. "You could have wished for a mansion, to get a job, hell, you could have even wished for me—another life. To be famous, have all the money you could spend, or even a bigger dick. But you wished for a fucking peach! I'm sick of waiting! I just got her to tell you the whole truth! Isn't that what you wanted?"

Her whole body was red now. It seemed like she was covered in blood.

"Do you know what happens when you make all your wishes, Justin?"

I was frozen, and a bird had my thumb in its mouth; I couldn't answer her.

"You get to be reborn." As she said this, she started floating like she did when she was going to kill Jeremi. Both arms spread out and hands up towards the sky. I said a prayer in my head, assuming that she was about to kill me just like she did to that asshole.

Suddenly, a cage appeared around her, and I could move again. The bird did not eat my thumb and just disappeared. The cage was large, domed like a bird cage, but made of dark metal. I tripped over myself and landed in the grass butt-first. There was a shadow that started to appear over me. My shoulders were grabbed in a grip that told me not to move.

"Don't move, Tin."

No fucking way. Tommy.

"Hey, Gabby," he said casually to the monster in the cage. "Long time no see."

Tommy was dressed like a cowboy. There was no other way to put it. The graying giant beard was the first thing I saw. He had on these big leather boots along with a vest. A huge belt that glimmered at me. His jeans had holes in them, and of course, he topped them off with a bright red, wide-brimmed hat. Talk about trying to look like a hero. Looking at my brother, I realized he had a wooden cane in his right hand. He started making his way towards Gabby, and I noticed his limp. His left leg seemed to no longer bend at the knee, and he relied extensively on the cane to assist him. I saw that the hand gripping the cane was missing the pinky. He was a Hand Bearer.

"So, Tin, it seems you've gotten into a situation." He said it calmly as if I wasn't thinking about how he was walking around *alive.*

"Our little friend Gabby here is more than you think. This isn't her first time being a Hand Bearer." He was looking up at her, screaming in the cage. She was floating around erratically like a bird that had just been caught.

My brother turned to me. He gave me a half smile as he folded his hands over the top of the cane together.

"As you can see, I am not dead. I did get hit by that truck and was pronounced dead at the scene. The last thing I remember was headlights and then being woken up by our lovely friend here." He pointed the cane at Gabby behind us. "She had something to do with me coming back to life."

"Why?" I asked. After I said that, I realized it could've come across as rude. He seemed like he just wanted to lecture me, though. We were never a family of formalities.

He laughed. "I don't know why. But afterward, she asked if I wanted wishes, and I said sure. I saw you at my funeral, along with Dad. I didn't want to make anything more complicated, so I just got a job as a horse trainer, which was as far away from here as possible."

That explains the cowboy get-up, I thought.

"But," he sighed, "I got this alert. I wished to know if there was ever violence toward you at this house, so I could come back and protect you."

Jesus, everyone had gone soft. My Gabby and Tommy—the only other people as cynical as I—had gone soft.

"Recently, I got a lot of alerts." He laughed. "Came as a

message through my radio station." He laughed again. "I figured you and Jeremi would bump heads once he bought our place. The first time, I was woken in the middle of the night, and the report I got said you got away from his gun. When I got this last one, though, I wished to be here. And thank fuck I did. Gabby isn't human, Tin; she's changed."

"I demand to be let out of here!" She yelled from her cage. The cage wavered a bit, but nothing happened. "I *wish* to be let out of here!" Her long nails screeched against the bars.

"Gabby used up her last wish to bring me back to life. I saw it. As you can see, her revival was not perfect because of this damn leg. Seven years ago, after I got hit, she was next to me at the morgue, and I remember waking up to her crying hysterically and yelling that she wished for me to come back and that it would make you love her. I saw a bright green flash, and then she was on the floor. Suddenly, her hair started floating around her, and her body stood up again.

"Looking at me with black eyes, she asked if I wanted her wishes. A huge knife appeared out of nowhere and cut my finger off. Once it was off, she ate it and went back to normal. I never asked her about it afterwards, because it seemed like she didn't recall it." Tommy lifted his left hand, which wasn't holding the cane. On his pinky was a nub of gold. He was also missing all of the other fingers on that hand now.

"I've only made four wishes. To be a horse trainer far, far away, to set that alert for you, to come back here, and to make that damn cage."

I was still too stunned to ask my brother anything. I didn't even know if I wanted to catch up with him. All I knew was that he knew more than I did, and Gabby was bad news.

"Kill you, kill you, kill you," Gabby was muttering to herself. The voice coming out seemed hers, and she wasn't floating around the cage.

"Our good friend here," Tommy said, looking me dead in the eye, "is a vessel for a demon, and it could be the man himself. Satan."

Chapter Seventeen

I must be dreaming, I thought, as Tommy and I walked inside our old house together, leaving Gabby outside to calm down and maybe become herself again.

The sudden memory of sitting on the curb not too far from here with Harley popped up in my head. *I need to make it right*, he said. With Satan? I was quiet, unsure how to take the news. These last few days had been anything other than usual, and I was too involved now. I almost wanted to run away, but I was done running.

Tommy explained to me, once we were inside and sitting on Jeremi's velvet sofa, that he was ashamed of himself and of our family, so he left. After rubbing his eyes out of exhaustion, he told me about the last night he was here. Dad had started to beat him, but he fought back for the first time. He then left Dad on his ass and ran. He always kept me in his thoughts, but I figured I would've been a baseball star by now.

"Maybe you are?" he said, giving me a side eye while looking at me in my big-ass fancy suit while raising an eyebrow.

"Nah, I'm not shit," I replied. Looking down at my shoes,

they were still dirty, reminding me where I belonged.

He continued to talk about how he found his love for horses and trained people to ride them. He vowed never to ride a motorcycle again. He had a wife he had met there and a kid waiting for him to come back home. I couldn't believe that I wouldn't have known he existed if he had never wished to return.

"Well, that's good to hear," he laughed and slapped me on the back. The boom of his laughter filled the empty house. I missed him and was surprised at how much I was feeling now.

"So what do you know about all this?" I held up my hands to reveal I was missing more fingers than he was.

"Well," he started, "after Gabby revived me, I found myself running out of the back of a morgue. Then, I made my first wish. When I wished to be far away, I ended up in Minnesota. Fresh in my reincarnated state, I went to the library and looked up anything related to wishes and fingers. I came across an ancient book called *One by One*. It was written during the Nordic Bronze Age, around 1750 BC. So many myths were coming out around that time, and much of what was written seemed to be fiction. The book described old Viking folklore about a spirit that would come at night and grant wishes to those who felt no hope left. Kind of like the tooth fairy, but taking your fingers, it needed a sacrifice," he wiggled his fingers on his lap. His hands were leathered like mine from the sun, but I could also see where the ropes left their marks.

"I read all I could about it and realized that once the wishes were up, there was something called 'revival.' There were multiple stories of people becoming devils or demons after being revived because it was 'against God's wishes.' It almost sounds like you lose a part of your soul to continue to live, like a deal with the devil. I found another book written soon after that that described different 'blood wishes.' It said that those with a certain lineage would have different wish capabilities. It came from three great kings at one point. The original Royal Hand Bearers. The special abilities that a select few could wish for were death, life, and love. I suspect Gabby might be from the lineage with the life-wishing aspect." He paused. I shook my head.

"She can wish for life. She wished for mine for the last revival. Normally, it is just a repeated revival of oneself. Like a strange loophole in a video game, you could also get revived more than once until the soul is depleted. It also seemed like each time, you got more possessed. Gabby over there has probably been revived more than once. On top of that, she revived me. Who knows who else she has revived? But it also goes the other way. There was also a statement that the last wish could be an ultimate 'death' for you or for someone you choose."

"How is that even fucking possible? Based on your *blood*?" I said in disbelief. I would be more skeptical if I hadn't witnessed Gabby kill someone right before my eyes. But...that wasn't her last wish.

"All of this *shouldn't* be possible. That's the thing. But with that cleaver, the curse still lives. The spirits that are trapped in it get stronger with each Hand Bearer. However, when the spirit eventually faded out of the culture of the society it was reaping in, it found an object to reside in. The cleaver is the source."

"Then what about the watch?" I asked.

"What watch?"

"The watch that stops time." I looked at his face for answers. It seemed that Tommy had somehow gotten smarter throughout the years. I was looking at a familiar stranger. He didn't wear all black and drown out the day with music anymore. It was weird to have a sense of trust in him, since he literally faked his death. Kinda.

"I have no fucking clue what you're talking about," he replied.

"Well, Gabby has one on her right now." I hoped she was back to normal.

We headed back outside, and the cage there looked like an abstract sculpture. Gabby was no longer in the cage.

"Shit. *Shit*. SHIT." Tommy kicked the ground. "Justin, she's going to go make more people Hand Bearers. We cannot let this happen. I also think she gains strength through the first wish."

I didn't know how many books Tommy read, but he seemed to learn the ins and outs of this she-devil situation. Gabby's car was still there, which was strange, but Tommy and I both looked at each other. I had hotwired a couple of cars back in New Mexico when I needed to go somewhere, and by the look on his face, I could tell he had done a couple of jobs himself.

Luckily, the car was unlocked, and Tommy gave me the honor of doing it because his leg was hurting. Damn, it's hard to hotwire with barely any fingers.

"Wait. You better with a gun or a sword?" I asked my brother.

"Uh, a gun?" I was glad he answered. I took off running back into the house. Having been there before, I knew all the weapons

Jeremi had stockpiled. The giant door that Candace had opened was still cracked. I guessed that Jeremi had been in a hurry to get out of there to hunt us. I pushed it back open. Shit. There were so many weapons. I hurriedly walked towards the wall of guns and grabbed a pistol for my brother because he seemed like he could only operate with one hand. I stepped over the pile of rubber ducks still on the floor and grabbed a couple of grenades and a purple, almost iridescent knife. It was probably only as long as my hand, including my fingers, but it had a good weight and nearly matched the purple on my pinky nub.

I looked to the right, and on the floor was the pile of rubber ducks again, just like we had left them. I almost felt bad, but the lady had also been trying to kill us, so she could have fun being a pile of ducks. I was turning to leave when I suddenly remembered Jeremi's uncle. I walked over to the small door and felt the blue glow. I left the weapons outside the room and crawled into it.

The man had changed positions. Instead of almost kissing his bloody hand like last time, he was angled in a way where he was almost in the fetal position. I entered his eyesight, and he slowly seemed to register my presence. He looked like he was moving in Jello.

"Uh, hi?" I said.

You shouldn't be here. Why did you come back? It was a man's voice in my head.

Unsure who was talking, I looked around the room. Lent's eyes followed me, and he didn't blink.

What are you looking for, asswipe? Is someone talking to you?

This was getting hostile, and I didn't know why I had ever come back.

You lost the girl. Too bad she was cute.

"So what?" I said.

She was also powerful, that's for sure. I wish my nephew had married her instead.

Disgusting, I thought.

As I approached the door to escape this stranger's berating, he said something that stopped me.

There's another cleaver.

I walked closer to him and stood with my arms crossed. He was moving slowly, but his eyes always stared into mine. He said the cleaver was supposed to be for Jeremi until he took over the company and stole all the relics Lent had found. The cleaver was in Lent's office on the other side of town. He wouldn't tell me exactly where it was because he wanted to make a deal.

What's in it for me? He said in my head.

"I have no idea what I could offer you, Lent. What do you want?" I asked.

He was quiet for a few minutes. I was about to leave the bastard there and find this cleaver myself, but he finally replied with a request I could have seen coming.

I want the girl.

I instantly felt my face get hot. No way was I going to let him even talk to Gabby again. Even if she was now a vessel for the devil, she was still a human. I hoped.

"Fuck you, Lent," I told him as I flicked his frozen nose.

His nose reacted; it had a weird ripple effect, and I left

before I could see the rest of him react. I crawled back through the space, grabbed the weapons I had collected, and headed back out into this fucked up world. I saw Tommy still sitting in the car, and I sat my happy ass into the driver's seat.

"There's another cleaver," I told him.

"Impossible," he stated in disbelief.

"I thought so, too, but let's get it before she does."

We both silently agreed, and I started to drive toward Lent's office.

Chapter
Eighteen

n the way to Lent's, getting caught up with my brother was nice. He invited me to see the ranch sometime after all this blew over. I thought the sentiment was nice, but I fucking hate horses. About twenty minutes in, I had a question burning at the tip of my tongue, so I figured I would just let the bullet fly.

"Have you talked to Mom at all?"

There was an empty silence after that. I felt the uneasiness set in like it always did, around the topic of our runaway mom.

"Tin. I have not," he replied in an oddly somber way. "I need to tell you something. I have been trying to avoid this for the rest of my life, but fate seems not to be that kind. I was awake on the night that Mom left. I ran into her in the kitchen, on my way to grab a cup of water. She was frantic and trying to pack anything and everything. I startled her when I asked her what she was doing."

I had my memories of this night, too. He paused and adjusted himself in the seat.

"Dad came down the stairs, too; he was drunk again, of course. Following her around the house. He was yelling and screaming at her to just fucking leave already. His eyes were dark, almost black, and he looked crazy. I couldn't get in between this time, like all the ones before, because Mom looked determined to fight back this time. When I was leaving the kitchen, I heard her scream at him, 'Fuck you.' Then I heard something that sounded like a vase breaking open. When I returned to the kitchen, Dad was standing over her."

Then the hammer dropped.

"Justin, Dad killed our mom."

It was so hard not to hit the brakes while I was driving. What the absolute fuck was going on? Why was the world I knew suddenly unraveling and tangling itself into this web of truths? I was shocked and didn't know what to say. Assuming he was telling the truth, I had to believe that my mother's time on Earth was cut so very short. Dad was an asshole anyway, and the story was believable. So I said the only thing I could.

"I hope that bastard rots in hell."

Tommy seemed to agree with this as he nodded and looked straight ahead.

"I'm sorry I never told you. As long as Dad was around, I was captive to his secret. He swore he would kill me next if you ever found out."

"As I said, I hope he rots in a burning shit pile in hell," I stated. My father was the worst. After Mom left—no, after he murdered her—he acted like the world was so peachy. Right before I was going to California, I had the last conversation I would ever have with him before his liver shut down. I remember him saying he was proud of me and that no one would ever understand all he had done for me. He would always say that, though. God, was this town corrupt or what?

"I don't want to talk about Mom anymore." I felt my eyes starting to blur. All the hate suddenly erupted from me. "But one more thing. Why didn't he get caught? Where the fuck is Mom's body?"

Tommy couldn't look at me.

"Tommy, what the fuck?"

"Dad buried her in the backyard. He told everyone she ran away and bought a storage locker to shove all of her shit into. Guess we'll never know where it is, though, since his will didn't say shit about it."

"Well, okay, how about this?" I suddenly realized. "How did you know Dad was dead?"

Tommy closed his mouth, puckered it like he had eaten something sour, and peered out the window. We were almost to Lent and Properties when he finally answered.

"Gabby told me."

There was an explosion from the building in front of us. The windows blew out and shattered along the sidewalk. Smoke started to billow from the top of the building, and Gabby stood on the roof in the shadows.

"Well, speak of the devil," I said. "We can talk about this later, but you can prove that you're on the right side by fighting with me. Right fucking now."

I handed him the pistol, which I trusted him to shoot

everyone but me with. I didn't know why he was still in contact with Gabby after she went crazy, bringing him back to life and all, but I hoped that he would still fight for the world to be free of this vessel for the devil, or maybe just a demon.

We hopped out of the car and looked up at Gabby. She looked like a mix between an angel and a villain. No wings adorned her back, but her hands were out like jetpacks. She floated down towards us; how nice of her.

"Gabby, stop this," I told her.

She started laughing. Again, the voice sounded like five people were laughing simultaneously. Her toes hit the hard ground yet gracefully.

"Oh, Justin, you were my favorite. It is a shame I have to get rid of you. It seems like you know too much now." She licked her lips as she was saying this and stared at me with black, soulless eyes.

The building behind her was now slowly falling apart. Big walls were collapsing on each other, and luckily, they seemed to be falling in the opposite direction from where we were. I could hear people's screams in the distance. The clouds of dust were coming our way anyway—fast.

I wonder where the fuck that cleaver is, I thought.

As if reading my mind, Gabby held up an object that glinted in the street light.

"Looking for this, fucker?"

She held up a cleaver that looked like the one I got my pinky cut off with. This one was a cool blue steel color, and when she held it up, it seemed to glow as she did.

“Well, come and get it.” She teased me with the cleaver. The layered voices sounded like an angry army asking for a fight. If she wanted a war, I would give her one.

“Okay, bitch, let’s dance.”

CHAPTER NINETEEN

hen Tommy and I were little, we would always fight each other. Mom had gotten us foam swords to play with since we had had an accident before. She said it was safer than plastic, Nerf guns, or even our fists. I knocked him on his ass so many times that he eventually complained to Mom that it was too easy for me to beat him up, so Mom took away our swords, and we were left with our imaginations. With no physical thing to destroy each other with, I came up with ways to outsmart him.

Since we were essentially playing "chase" after that, I would hide from him, trip him with sticks he didn't see coming, or insult him with my words to distract him. As we got older, we would wrestle, and in middle school, a couple of times, we got into fights because we were both bullied so badly. It never got *too* bad, though, usually just shoving and yelling. That said, Tommy and I had never been in a real fight in our lives, except for one that went too far.

I don't know what the hell I was thinking of, challenging Gabby.

She darted towards me from below the building, and debris followed in her wake. She was like a shadow being shot like an arrow. I grabbed a grenade I had in my pocket, and if video games had taught me anything, this was my moment to shine. Not thinking but acting in the moment, I removed the grenade's pin and threw it straight at Gabby. I guess I wasn't concerned that it would kill her, since she wasn't human anymore. But while I watched it fly slowly towards her, I thought of Tommy and me. And I fucked up. We were going to get blown to shreds.

"I wish Tommy and I were 3,000 feet away to the right!" I uttered, as Gabby caught the grenade I threw at her.

Everything happened fast and slow all at once. I had made the wish, and my hands lifted like they always did; time slowed. I took a second to look around me. Gabby was screaming still, her face stuck in a demented half-expression of pure terror, and my brother Tommy was looking at her with his gun pointed in her direction. But his eyes were black. Before I could stop any of it, an ant trail led up my arm. My right ring finger quickly turned dark, and ants crawled on it until there was no finger left to see. Then it was all gone. I felt the back of my shirt get pulled fast and hard. We moved through a tunnel that felt like we were dragged through a Disneyland hallway. Until there was a quick 'pop' and Tommy's eyes were back to normal, and I was staring at a substantial fucking dent in the earth.

With no sign of Gabby, I walked over to Tommy. We were both perfectly fine, but that didn't stop Tommy.

He hit the back of my head really hard. “Way to go, dumbass.”

For a second, it was just like we were little again. My brother was by my side, and we were up to no good. I smiled for a second until I remembered.

“Hey, Tommy. When I made that wish, I thought your eyes were black like Gabby’s for a second.”

He got beet red.

“Oh, that’s weird.” He tried an awkward laugh. “I can assure you I am not like her, dude.”

He said it in a way that was suspicious to me, but also, we had just destroyed a good portion of the town, so I was also thinking of getting the hell out of there.

“Okay, well, we should leave in case Gabby returns.”

And speaking of the damn devil. A piercing screech came from a pile of debris about fifty feet away. Gabby’s body was demented; her arm was twisted in a way that she almost looked like a doll that a kid had manipulated into the most uncomfortable position ever.

She started hobbling towards us while cracking her bones back into place. Her eyes were the darkest black I had ever seen, and her skin was ruby red. Her hair was white and floating. I knew that this was her most dangerous state. Full Satan mode.

“I’m sick of playing all your stupid little games, Justin.” She cracked her neck back into place. “We could have this all for ourselves.” She motioned to the open air around her.

“I could give you everything you ever wanted. I gave you back, Tommy, see?” She pointed with a broken finger that straightened out slowly. It was as if the real Gabby was talking, but it wasn't her.

"Bastard." I heard him mutter under his breath.

I felt like I was caught in a bad place with a tough choice. I had to choose my crazy ex-girlfriend or my should-be-dead brother. I grabbed the knife I had hidden in the small of my back and was getting ready for Gabby to swing one of her talons at me, but all of a sudden, I heard a footstep behind me, and then everything went black.

CHAPTER TWENTY

abby was one of those girls who didn't believe in receiving flowers. When we first started dating, I would bring her some whenever I thought of it, and always got the same response: 'Why, they're just going to die.'

I tried not to let it hurt me so much. I imagined a life where I could spoil my significant other in ways I never saw my parents spoil each other, even if it was just flowers. I continued to bring them to her, and I still got the same response every time. The last time I got her flowers was when she was supposed to leave.

"Don't do this, Justin," she told me with her hands up. "I don't know why you keep doing this."

"Because I love you."

The answer was so simple and pure.

My head hit what felt like the door of a car, and I opened my eyes to see a blurry vision of Tommy driving Gabby's car. I was in the backseat, off to Tommy's right. I tried to reach up to rub my forehead where the pain was. I couldn't move my fucking hands.

They were tied together, and there was also a cloth shoved in my mouth and tied behind my head. I kept blinking to clear my vision. One thing that hadn't changed was that Tommy knew how to shut a man up.

"Rise and shine, my lovely," Tommy said. Something in his voice changed. It felt like he was no longer warm towards me, and that statement felt like ice was being thrown at me.

I could already piece the puzzle together. Gabby and Tommy were working together, and for some reason, I was the target, and now I was going to get dragged to God knows where, and they were going to fucking skin me alive or some shit. I shouldn't have trusted him. I had seen enough movies and read enough crime stories. I figured it was what I deserved.

"It looks like you saw me for who I am," Tommy said, looking at me and back at the road. All of a sudden, his voice seemed to get softer. "I'm a demon."

I saw his hands shift from a white-knuckled grip on the car's wheel to a relaxed position. With the cloth in my mouth, I couldn't say anything, and with all this shit going on, a demon was expected. I made some muffled noise in reaction since he was waiting for it.

"Oh, right, I tied you up," he said as if he had forgotten. I looked out the window to see a small town. I saw the lights of a Jack in the Box and knew we were at least in some civilization.

"Please don't be mad at me, Justin." Looking back at me with clear blue eyes, he said, "Gabby did this to me."

No shit. I thought and rolled my eyes.

"When she made the wish for me to come back to life and went all gold and shit, I think it transferred some power to me. Demonic power. After all those years, she used her last finger to wish me back to life. But she already was the vessel for Satan when she revived me, since she shouldn't be able to revive anyone but herself. That's what happened, and that's why I'm screwed up. Or-maybe it's the way the finger is cut off. Haven't you thought about that?"

He asked a silent crowd. What he said was interesting, though; I had never thought what would happen if I were to use all my fingers. The purple may mean something else. Maybe Gabby cutting off my first finger would have a strange effect later. I just thought that I'd get my fingers back.

"Well, anyway, that bastard made me a fucking weirdo, and now I go through phases of blacking out and doing evil shit. Like tying you up. It got worse when she was around, and I didn't want you to notice, so I knocked you out."

As much as I wanted to believe Tommy, a nagging voice still told me Gabby was good. She was good, right?

Tommy pulled over on the side of the road and started untying me. We were standing in dirt so dry it could've been dust. I could feel how sorry he was, and I understood he did the best thing he could at the time, but now I didn't know where Gabby was. What should my next step be?

"I'm sorry about this, buddy. I don't even know where we are." He rubbed his nose and looked around.

I hated that my first thought was to send us back to New Jersey.

Once the cloth was out of my mouth, I asked him my burning question.

"So what happened to Gabby?"

He looked down at the floor.

"After I knocked you out, she was so surprised. I turned the pistol on her next. She turned to me and said a couple of words that sounded like a spell, and then I blacked out. The next thing I knew, I was driving, and you were still passed out in the backseat. I figured I was driving to get away from Gabby, but also, I have no fucking clue what she told me to do. I could be taking you to the place she wants you to be. Might be more dangerous, who knows?"

He sounded defeated but also relieved.

"That's why I gotta leave you, Tin."

What the fuck?

"I can't let her get close to me again, and somehow, if I end up killing you, man... I can't do that. I can't fucking do that. Maybe she commanded me to kill you in two hours. You know how it would go, you remember Dad."

The flashback was vivid and fast.

It was the first and only fight we had been in. We were outside, and Dad was smoking a cigar. I must've only been around 6; Tommy was 11. He handed Tommy a small knife, and I got his trusty pocket knife.

"Good boys," he said through the fog of whiskey, "Now play."

At first, it was fun. Tommy and I acted like we were in a sword battle—until Dad got mad and got behind Tommy.

"Let me show you how to do it, son." He grabbed Tommy's hand, and as if showing him how to play pool, he drew his hand back, and before I could react, my shoulder was bleeding like crazy. I remember looking up and seeing Tommy trying to hold back his tears. My father's face was dark and twisted, but his teeth seemed to glow from the smile he possessed. I ran inside soon after, and Mom found out. That's when Tommy and I were told we weren't allowed to fight anymore. She gave us foam swords and locked the knives away. We didn't see Dad for a couple of days after that.

Looking at Tommy in the present, I saw the scared little boy. It was taking too much out of him to be in the crossfire, especially if I was there.

"I understand," I said as I nursed my bruised wrists. I patted him on the back. "Don't fuck anything else up."

The green in his eyes got brighter as a tear tried to escape.

"I'll call you," he said.

I laughed. "I don't have a damn phone."

"Oh, right. Then you call me."

He gave me his home phone number and address, wished me luck, and told me to escape this place. He shoved two hundred dollars in my hand as he shook it goodbye. I would've gone with him if he had offered, but he didn't. I guess that was fine; for some reason, I was Gabby's only target.

He got in the car, rolled down the passenger window, started the engine, and looked at me.

"I love you, Tin."

"Love you too, man."

It was so pure and simple. I looked down and saw a dandelion. I picked it up and made a wish. I blew out the seeds like a candle. Out of all the flowers, that was Gabby's favorite. Maybe that's why she never liked the flowers I gave her. I had a weird feeling that it was the last time I'd see my brother.

Fuck.

Chapter
Twenty-One

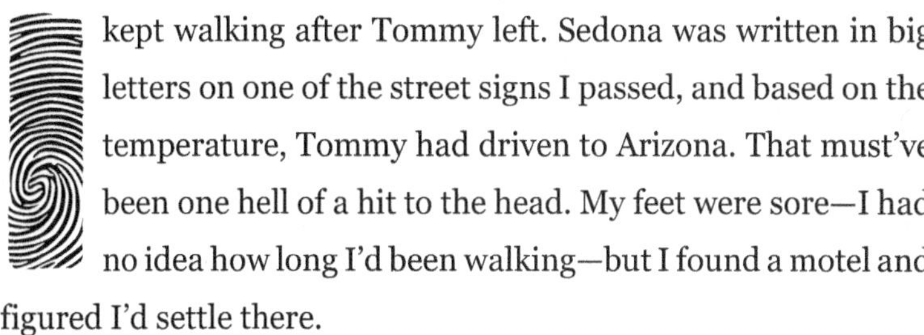

I kept walking after Tommy left. Sedona was written in big letters on one of the street signs I passed, and based on the temperature, Tommy had driven to Arizona. That must've been one hell of a hit to the head. My feet were sore—I had no idea how long I'd been walking—but I found a motel and figured I'd settle there.

Walking up to the lady at the front desk, I started to take out the money Tommy had given me.

"One night stay, please," I said, trying not to sound defeated.

"Alright, hun." She handed me some keys. "Sixth floor, room 666."

She seemed to smirk when she said it. Her gray hair was frayed everywhere, and she looked like a classic old lady witch. Short and stumpy, kind of like a pumpkin. I was trying not to think too hard about it or the fact that my room was the devil's number.

I went up to the sixth floor and got into my room. Immediately, I fell upon my bed, and the day's weight sank into the moldy-smelling sheets. I kept having flashes of Tommy's face with black eyes and then without. I was trying to figure out how these fingers fucking work. I only had so many left that I couldn't waste them. I wondered if I was the only Hand Bearer who knew the ins and outs of the gross operation that Lent and Properties was carrying out. I felt like a martyr. A spokesperson. A team captain. I hated it.

In baseball, I used to be the pitcher. I could throw a ball as fast as 95 miles an hour by age 18. I was elected team captain because I got along with everyone, and I was pretty damn good at the game. So many colleges were scouting me out, and people often joked that I could put all their names in a hat and pick one. I felt like I was a winner on top of the world.

I met Jasmine at an orientation for one of the top colleges in California that I was considering. She was a blond bombshell who kept staring at me the entire time. I wasn't expecting to hit it off with her, but we talked about sports 'cause she played volleyball. We spent the rest of orientation laughing and joking about random ass shit. It was during a time when Gabby and I were talking about going away to college and how long-distance would work, and she was never optimistic about it. I felt like I had an opportunity to have my first college experience, which was cheating on my girlfriend. What an asshole I am.

I fell asleep to the dripping of the sink, wishing to return to New Mexico before that happened.

I woke up before the sun was up. I had stayed in the same position all night, and I felt on high alert. I almost assumed that at any moment, Gabby would burst into the room and kill me with her words. Or cut me to bits with the new cleaver she had, and I'd be a demon. I kinda wondered why I wasn't dead already. One thing was evident when I woke up, though. And that was that I had to stop Gabby.

It was four in the morning, and I figured it was time to start the day since I couldn't fall asleep. I grabbed my suit coat and headed towards the motel's entrance to see if there was any breakfast I could grab quickly. The witch lady was awake and seemed to be putting some little baggies out for me, so I took one and started to walk out.

"Justin," the old lady's voice called out.

I turned around so fast, I could almost swear I had sprained my neck.

"Did you sleep well?"

"How the fuck do you know my name?"

"It's on the check-in sheet, dear." She answered with that weird smirk again. Her face was wrinkled and worn. She wore the same clothes as yesterday but had added an apron. She looked familiar in a way that reminded me of my mother.

"I slept like shit, thanks for asking. Now I have to go. Have a good day, witch."

I threw in that last part because I felt like I'd never see her again, and someone had to let her know that her outfit made it seem like it was Halloween.

She started almost laughing, but more like cackling, as I walked away.

Weird ass bitch. I thought.

I walked until I found a bus stop a few blocks down and waited for it to take me away somewhere. I looked down at my hands and felt sad. These were wishes that I was supposed to make until I was found and killed for the rest of them. For a split second, I thought of wishing them all at once to get it over with. I felt like I was being watched, though. With how long Gabby had been in the game, I was sure she probably had eyes all over. One of them could have been that old witch.

Someone had come up and stood beside me, but I hadn't noticed until they started talking.

"Where are you headed?"

A small woman, probably in her 40s, stood close to me. Her hair was blond and messy, but she wore a pantsuit. We were almost matching. Maybe she was a lawyer.

"Anywhere but here," I replied.

She laughed and looked down at the dirt. I shoved my hands in my pockets just in case she was another Harley.

"You know the bus doesn't arrive until 6, right?" she said, looking at me. I felt her eyes go up and down my body. First, I was flustered; she was checking me out but had nothing else to say. But I realized she was probably wondering whether I was going to work or to an event, since it was so early in the morning and I was in a fucking war-torn suit. I saw the giant mark on my white suit shirt from the dirt I must've fallen on when Tommy hit me.

"Shit." That was all I could muster out.

"Do you want to grab a drink?" she asked.

"Sure."

Probably not the smartest choice to get a drink with a stranger after all that I have been through, but fuck it. We ended up going back to the motel where I stayed. There was a small section that looked like it had once been a restaurant but had since become a bar. There was someone at the counter, so we headed inside. Little did I know that my good friend, the witch lady, was also the bartender.

“Fancy seeing you again, “ she greeted me and looked at the friend I had brought along. “And your lovely lady.”

We both said a half-hearted hello to the stranger.

I ordered a rum and coke with whatever money Tommy had left me, and she got a vodka cranberry.

She was instantly taken aback when I took my hands out of my pockets.

“W-What happened to you?” Her face seemed to shrink up with disgust.

“Poked around in places I shouldn’t have.”

I thought I was hilarious, offering these half-assed replies to those who asked me. But it was early enough that I almost felt like being honest.

When the motel lady returned, I read her name tag and saw that it said Linda. She gave us our drinks and then shuffled back to the breakfast area to continue handing out bags of whatever. I forgot. I had grabbed one and left it at the bus stop.

“I’ll be back real quick,” I said and turned to go. My bus stop friend seemed to take this the wrong way.

“Why are you leaving me?”

I felt a very tight, powerful grip around my wrist. Her eyes were black. Her drink was gone, and I felt the room start spinning.

Shit.

I tried to jerk my arm away from her, but her fingers tightened. Her eyes were black.

"Justin, come, play."

I was being hunted now. I couldn't go anywhere or trust anyone. I looked at my fingers and tried to think of a good wish to make. I could wish for her to turn into something. I would want to be somewhere else. I could wish for the fucking world to end.

Her face looked like Candace's when she was holding that shotgun. The shark smile could have been copied and pasted. My new bus stop friend was a fucking demon, and that realization sent a shiver down my spine, making me feel a mix of fear and fascination.

I saw a whiskey glass sailing through the air and landing perfectly on her temple, and she was knocked out.

My eyes followed to the counter, and Linda stood in the perfect form of a final pitch.

"Thank you," I said, stumbling over the words, regretting being a little mean towards her.

"No problem. We Hand Bearers need to look out for one another." She winked and wiggled her fingers in front of her face. She was missing two fingers on her right hand. Her pinky was orange. How had I not noticed it?

"Whoa, whoa, whoa," I started walking towards her to make sure it wasn't a trick of the light. "What the *fuck*."

"You probably don't recognize me; I wished to be unrecognizable. I was thinking of witches around Halloween, so I think they—" she looked up to the sky— "took some liberties with that. But it's nice to see you again," she smiled at me, revealing the demon-like features that made her unrecognizable.

I sat back down; my chair was still warm, and what Linda said next changed my entire view on this shit.

"I'm sure you've already run into my daughter. You two were always inseparable. It's me, Rose. Gabby's mom."

CHAPTER TWENTY-TWO

"She told me you were dead," I started.

Rose had made us coffee to wake up, although I didn't need to wake up after being fucking attacked. We sat at the bar where I had just shared a drink with the lady still lying on the ground, out cold. We tied her up just in case she decided to come back to life with that fiery rage. She had no missing fingers, so I thought she had been cut with the cleaver and had those harmful effects.

"Sounds like my girl, always lying," she bittersweetly smiled. "She was always such a driving force in this world. It's no wonder she got involved in such a huge global scheme."

"Global?" I asked. This thing was bigger than I thought.

"Oh, you didn't hear?" Her smile turned into a flat line, just like my heartbeat. "Lent and Properties just bought some buildings in Canada and Taiwan. They are spreading faster than a fire in summer," she said, and a chill ran through me, making me feel the weight of a looming global threat.

I felt like my jaw hit the floor. These people were trying to involve the whole world. That would be unlimited wishes forever.

Also, Jeremi was dead, so who the fuck was running the scheme now?

"There's also something about these colors," she held up her hand with the pinky nub, an iridescent orange. "They mean something. I think it's correlated with how much power your wishes have. Or perhaps the intensity with which they are granted. And I have never seen your color before."

I looked down at my sad-looking hands. The color of my pinky seemed less intense, but it was still shimmery. I wondered what color was the most powerful. Some of me wanted to say Gabby was the proud owner of the most powerful, but that freaked me out.

Tommy had said something about this; I remembered something about three kings. Perhaps the color was a lineage of sorts.

"I've seen a couple of Hand Bearers come through here," she continued, "Many of them only had one or two wishes left. Most of them were orange or red. It seems that many Hand Bearers use their wishes quickly. I guess that's almost better...so they don't get hunted." She looked at me, then looked away.

"I think they're after you. I think your wishes are stronger than you think," she declared to me. I felt like I was the chosen one again. A Harry Potter in this world because this didn't feel fucking real. It was wrong for me to convince myself of any of that. But looking around, I now knew this place was full of demons and chaotic wishes that maybe had a bigger picture than what I was seeing because they wanted the world to count down. On their fingers. Waiting for your wishes. Fuck.

"Gabby gave me these," she said, looking sadly at her fingers. "She was caught up with Jeremi, and five years ago, she went on a rampage. I was one of her lucky picks. After she screamed at me to leave, I wished to look completely different, so I hopped on a bus and ended up here. I haven't made any more wishes. I want to be careful."

I understood her thought process: given her state, dealing with Gabby made her want to leave, but I couldn't understand how easily she gave up. I remembered her being firm with Gabby growing up and setting the rules straight. She looked defeated now, but maybe that was just the disguise.

I should probably get going, I thought, looking around. If one person attacked me, who knew if there would be more?

"Well, it was great talking to you, Rose, but I think I have to head out. I don't know who might be after me now." I pointed awkwardly at the woman resting on the floor.

"Can I come with you?" Rose squeaked out.

I had to think fast about this. This was Gabby's mom. Having her around might make Gabby angrier, especially if she thought Rose was dead. Or maybe she knew she was still alive, since Gabby lied to me so much. It would be nice to have some company, and it seemed like she had some information on her fingers. I felt like I was picking my team for the next Mystery Gang.

"Sure," I told her as I got up and put on my suit coat. "I don't know where the fuck I'm going, though."

"I think we have to go back to New Jersey," she already sounded exhausted.

"I guess so."

"You were going to take the bus?"

"I guess so."

"I think I can do one better." She winked when she said it, and her hand floated up before her. Unlike before, I could see what was happening to her finger this time. Her right hand grabbed the dull dining knife on the table. Her left hand was still in front of her. With one fluid motion, the blade sliced through the left index finger on the top part of the counter, and it landed with a *plop* in her coffee below. *Nasty*.

Immediately, we were teleported through a jello tube and spit out right in front of Avondale. I guessed this was the place Rose remembered best since her house wasn't hers anymore.

"Well, now where?" I asked Rose.

"We hunt Gabby."

CHAPTER TWENTY-THREE

ose and I walked to my old house, unsure of where to start. I figured since Jeremi was for sure dead, the rest of his family was missing, and his uncle was frozen, it could be our safe house while we decided what to do next.

"I always liked you, Justin," Rose said as we walked. She walked a little slower, but we were side by side, taking one step at a time. "But I never understood why you went to California."

Oh great, here we go again. I thought.

I felt like I had already gone through all this with Gabby: the cheating, the moving, and then the eventual doom end of my life.

"I guess it was just something I had to do." I felt like I was being blamed.

"But just for a girl?"

I was stunned. I wasn't expecting to be grilled like this. I was stuck, and it felt like my own mom was cornering me.

"Even after everything you and Gabby went through?" She stopped in the middle of the sidewalk and turned to me. Gently, she said, "Even the baby?"

What fucking baby? I thought.

"What?" I stopped walking, too. I needed to hear what she was about to say. In my prom suit and having barely slept, I was ready to face the whole truth of my past.

"The baby. Gabby told me you didn't want it, so she ended up giving the baby away to be adopted. I believe Jeremi adopted the sweet girl."

Why did I have no memory of this? Why was this the first time I was hearing that I had a fucking *child?* Was I a father? Could my life get any more chaotic and out of my control?

I vaguely remembered the last conversation I had with Gabby before I left. We stood outside her house, and I brought her flowers for the last time. She took them and had tears in her eyes the whole time. I told her I had met someone else, and it would be best if we parted ways. She was silent the entire time. Maybe I never gave her the time to say what she needed. I had an awful thought soon after.

The baby was the devil-looking thing that I sent to an orphanage.

I felt like I could puke.

Seeing how I was reacting, Rose stopped talking so I could process for a second. She put her hand on my shoulder. Her touch was firm but reassuring.

"I'm so sorry. I thought she would have told you. That's why she didn't leave here. When you came back from touring, she found out. She said she told you, and you got so angry that you would leave with a new girl."

I guess the flowers I gave her after that conversation were disposed of, the peanut gallery of my brain offered.

My heart felt like it had been ripped out. Not only had Gabby wished for my life to be miserable, but she kept my daughter from me, and now I would never get to see her. Part of me was wondering why Gabby didn't say anything or fucking stop me from sending our daughter away.

"I can't believe you never knew," Rose said, letting the last word linger. My anger for Gabby was brewing. I remember feeling like I could fall in love with her again. Not anymore. I declared war against Gabby and her stupid Hands. We walked in silence for the rest of the way.

We got to my old house, and just like I had suspected, no one was there. Rose said she'd go inside, and I wanted to wait outside in the cold for a bit to contemplate all the information I'd had thrown at me. I had to make a plan. I sat down in the grass. It was slightly wet, as the sprinklers had just gone off, but I didn't care.

I could only think about that little girl's eyes when she saw us. They were a brilliant green like Gabby's eyes before turning red. I wondered if she held the secret to stopping Gabby. Based on how she reacted when confronted with her in the house, Gabby was at a standstill. Maybe she was afraid of the kid. If I hadn't done anything, I was unsure if Gabby would have. I replayed that moment and saw my life flash before me with different paths I could have taken—the one where I knew about the kid and the one where I didn't.

I looked down at the wishes I had left and figured that I could at least try to be a dad now. I looked around at the yard that

I used to play in with my brother, and the house my family had lived in. It was strange deciding to become a family man all of a sudden.

"I wish the little girl I banished to an orphanage would return here."

A bald eagle came out of nowhere, swooped down, and landed on my left hand. The massive bird didn't feel heavy. Its beak started to wrap around my ring finger, and I watched my finger go inside its mouth. The eagle didn't look bothered, and clamped its beak down at the base of my finger. No snap of my fingers was heard, and I swear I heard it chirp, 'Wish granted,' as it flew back into the tree in the front yard and disappeared.

Suddenly, I was face-to-face with a little girl whose name I didn't even know.

CHAPTER TWENTY-FOUR

It's Beth."

She glared at me. We were sitting across from each other on the grass. Her little fingers, which were all intact, were twirling the strands of grass around and poking the bugs that walked by. Happy as she was no longer in a sad orphanage, she couldn't care less about where her parents had gone.

"Mommy was never nice to me," she said when I told her her parents were gone. "Neither was Daddy."

"I understand that," I told her, and picked a blade of grass that she had ripped out. A flash of my father's face came to my mind. He ripped out the 'for sale' sign from where I was sitting now. "This used to be my house."

She looked up at the house. Her eyes were green, for now, and she took in the outside of the house as if she was memorizing it for a painting, hardly blinking.

"I know," she said. "You're Justin."

Shocked, but also not too shocked, as this damn world was falling apart as I spoke.

"And what do you know about me, kid?"

She stared at me, her eyes seeming to peer into my soul. I felt like I could not lie to her. She was this oracle child; she was my child.

"You are a *loser.*"

I started laughing. I could only think of how many times Jeremi must have told her I sucked that she got the message. It was the first time in this experience that I felt a release of emotions. Like a dam finally opening, the laughter turned into tears, and I sobbed like a mess. *Damn, when did I get so soft?*

"You are also my father." Beth offered my tears when she saw them. She seemed like a nice girl with just a sprinkle of evil. "My real father."

My heart started to beat fast because I was nervous about asking her this next question. I sniffled and pulled myself together really fucking quick.

"Do you know who your mother is? Your real mom?"

"The mom that gave me up? Yeah. You guys came. I saw. I thought you would take me with you. Batty and I."

My heart sank. We were too busy trying to get the fuck out of that house. I didn't even consider what she thought was happening. She was for sure angry, though.

"Do you know why your eyes turn red?" I asked her. I wasn't expecting her to know what was going on. At best, maybe she knew what a Hand Bearer was.

"They get red because I'm a demon. Mommy is a demon. So was Mister Jeremy and Candace."

She said it matter-of-factly, as if I were the one who didn't know what was happening. I allowed her to think that so that I could ask her more questions.

"What did Mister Jeremi do?"

She started from the beginning—or at least what she remembered. Jeremi had taken her in once Gabby had decided that parenthood was not her thing. She was always at Jeremi's house, but Gabby chose to leave around the time Beth was six months old. Beth would stay at the house with Candace, who would try to teach her a form of homeschooling when she was growing up—essentially Wishing Hands 101.

Beth knew she was a devil when she started her terrible twos and demanded things left and right. Sometimes, if she wanted it hard enough, the thing would happen. For example, if she wanted a cookie, she could get frustrated enough to demand it, and it would happen just like Gabby had demanded Jeremi's death. Our favorite person, Jeremi, was teaching her to be a Finger Reaper. It was her main goal in life. She also said she would have liked to have wishes, but thought that killing someone for them was 'pointless.' She even knew about the watch, the cleaver, and all the weapons. She was only eight, but talking to her felt like she was almost a teenager. She told me that her life wasn't just learning about Finger Reaping; Jeremi and Candace also made her do so many chores, and she currently had a charity in her name because Jeremi had convinced some fucker that she had a long-term disease. Little did they know it was just devil-ism.

"Mommy's getting stronger." Her little voice seemed to recoil.

"Mommy used to visit a lot more. She would come by and take me to the market. I got to pick out fruit." She smiled, but it was awkward as she sported little pointy teeth.

"She is so strong, she wants to kill me." I offered her a sly smile.

"Well, yeah," she said, touching my hand, "You have purple."

At the same time, Rose had come out of the house holding two mugs of what I'm assuming was more coffee. Rose loves her coffee. Once she saw the child, she stopped in her tracks.

"Who's that?" Beth asked me.

It clicked that Rose was in disguise, so even if Beth saw her, she wouldn't recognize her now. And it might be the first time they had met.

"She's a very good friend of your mother's," I offered. Rose strolled towards us, never taking her eyes off Beth. "It's okay, Rose, we're just talking."

"Rose is my favorite flower," Beth offered to a nonexistent conversation.

Rose wept as she handed me my coffee and sat down with us in the grass. The sun was setting again, and we all needed to get some rest soon. I decided I'd only drink half of my coffee.

"You've gotten so big," Rose said, forgetting Beth wouldn't recognize her. So they had met.

I took a sip of my coffee.

"SHIT," I yelled, "That's hot as fuck!"

"That's hot as fuck!" Beth echoed back at me.

Oh, so this is what it's like to have kids.

Chapter Twenty-Five

y mind was stuck on the color purple. Harley and I had laughed about it, but that felt like years ago, instead of days.

Beth and Rose introduced themselves, and I could feel Rose's heartbreak as she realized I had wished for her to return. I don't think she knew I wished she were gone in the first place. I would blame Gabby for that fuck up. Rose took Beth inside to clean her up and get her changed into something that wasn't the orphanage dress.

I paced around the velvet-covered living room, which looked much like it had when I lived there. Of course, my father's chair wasn't there, but I could feel his presence. I thought of Jeremi's uncle in the basement. I wondered if he was still there.

For a second, I wanted to think about my father. He had always told Tommy and me how blessed he was. How we would never understand the things he did. I remember hearing him yell at my Mom over and over again, and arguing about work. About his protection. About our protection. I hadn't looked up his company in a while. I knew my dad was a realtor of some sort. I hopped onto Jeremi's computer. The ballsack had not set a password, so I searched for what I could remember. My heart dropped.

Many years ago, my father's company was just a couple of real estate agents starting out. Among his coworkers were men with greater dreams and stronger desires. Looking into the pictures and history, one guy's name kept popping up. Lent. Lent and Properties was a business that a couple of people from my dad's company started. My dad was in the picture with Lent, signing the company paperwork. My dad and Lent were coworkers. *Oh fuck no.*

I looked up to see Rose walking towards me, and I told her the news.

"My dad and Lent used to work together."

She made a sound that made me assume she understood the weight of the comment.

"I knew he always had something fishy about him," she said.

I patted myself down to find Tommy's note with his number on it. I called Rose on his phone and told him the news.

"Well, that explains a lot."

"What the fuck do you mean by that, Tommy?"

Being older than me, Tommy could see more clearly when Dad got involved with Lent. Tommy recalled that Lent gave him a gold watch and told him to keep it safe and hidden. It happened around the time that I was 14 and Tommy was 18. I thanked God Tommy was an excellent eavesdropper, because I couldn't recall Dad ever having that gold watch.

"You remember him telling us that he was a blessing?"

"Yeah. One giant pile of shit blessing." Tommy said.

I kept clicking on articles and news stories, one after the other.

"They both were a part of the company's start and called themselves the 'Wishing Angels.' Dad must've thought that he was somehow actually doing good. But that was the start of the corruption. They met with angry mobs of people and investors, and eventually had to shut down the original company they had formed. It was called 'Giving Hands'. After the backlash, Lent re-named it. This company has been around longer than we thought."

The company started around the time we moved here. I assumed my father had no other job and met Lent pretty fast. It started a few years before we moved, so perhaps they knew each other growing up. I couldn't believe my father was best friends with my bully's father, and I never knew.

An image of the whole world getting involved in this crazy finger scheme appeared in my head. The whole damn world. They would take money from strangers to grant wishes for success or to find a missing child. At this point, the company was at least 25 years old. I thought about the kids. Were they getting fingers, too? Or only the lowlifes like me?

Tommy and I also discussed the colors of our pinkies. If his was fucking *gold,* then what the hell was my purple? If anything, I would have thought gold was the most powerful, but he seemed to disagree.

"I've thought about this before," he started, "I think...I think it has to do with what I read about. The four main colors I read about were red, pink, purple, and green. They all have some trace-ability back to when the lore was first found. Remember those kings I told you about? There were only three of them. Yurt, Pisne, and Trili," he paused for a second. "They were brothers, and the tale of the cleaver stems from a rumor one faraway kingdom heard. This shit show all came from a servant. Pisne's servant found the cleaver hidden in a jar coming from Trili's territory overseas; he accidentally cut himself. This servant was the first to receive the blessings of the cursed souls."

"So, he was a demon?" I asked. All I could think of was how he compared the cleaver to the tooth fairy earlier. Should've just said the cleaver was a bringer of chaos.

"Not really. Since he was the first blood that the cleaver tasted, and it was not strong enough, having no souls yet, he went to show King Pisne." He continued, "After a day of looking at this cleaver that was assumed to be a gift from his brother, he decided to chop some meat with it. It was a pig, apparently, and once he chopped off a foot of the pig, the cleaver started glowing."

"So then the pig was a demon?" I asked, trying not to laugh.

"Fuck no, listen to me, Justin." He was getting annoyed. "That's when the cleaver revealed itself to Pisne. It asked for more sacrifice. Like Gabby's voice, it was layered. King Pisne referred to the cleaver as the 'Warrior.'"

He started talking faster. "Pisne noticed the foot he had just chopped off was gone. He assumed that the Warrior had taken it as part of the sacrifice. He agreed to give him more of a sacrifice after the cleaver had told him that it needed more and plunged the cleaver deep into the pig's heart. The writing states that the pig disappeared and Pisne was blessed with a red pinky."

Fuck.

Pisne was intrigued and impressed, and he visited his brothers by boat. He went to the kingdom of Yurt first. His kingdom was known for its great wealth in plants and agriculture. All of his crops thrived. After discussing what happened to the pig with his brother, there was no answer to what had happened. They assumed that Trili had found witchcraft, which at that time was frowned upon. They both agreed that it had been sent it to Pisne to hide. After they went to bed that night, Pisne snuck out of his chambers and visited Yurt in his room. While still asleep, the cleaver whispered for another sacrifice. Pisne chopped off his brother's whole hand." He stopped.

"Tommy, what the fuck. They didn't have a watch or anything, so why would it work?" I wanted to know the answer.

"That's why I was confused when you brought up that stupid watch. I don't think they need it. Perhaps a tactic to make sure no one else can see. Or an escape plan if they get caught. It sounds like they can escape death with that thing, so I think that came much later. The thing is, you don't need the watch."

I was stunned. Too stunned to ask him any more questions right now.

"So, then what?" I sat back in my chair, ready for the next set of 'impossible shit that happened' to come at me.

"Yurt, of course, woke up due to his brother's decision. However, there was no blood. The cleaver was glowing again, and from the hand he had left, his pinky disappeared and left a green mark. The sacrifice was accepted. Yurt flew into a fit of rage since Pisne had just crippled him, and he needed his hands to be a good farmer. Pisne was banished from Yurt's kingdom that night."

I sympathized with Yurt, as he hadn't chosen for that to happen to him. Also, his fucking brother did that to him. Whereas my dumbass agreed to those wishes in a second.

"Pisne then went to Trili's kingdom. It was over the long sea, and his kingdom was known for fishing. Pisne was the king of trade, essentially, so he and Trili had always had a better relationship than his other brother. When Pisne got there, he explained everything to Trili. Trili was confused, as he had not sent the cleaver. Not knowing shit about the cleaver or what it was capable of, Trili asked Pisne to leave before anything else happened. Pisne resisted and got angry. The cleaver had spoken to him again, getting stronger with each sacrifice; he lunged at his brother. Pisne was able to get a cut in Trili's thigh and severed a main artery. This was when Trili's pinky disappeared, and bystanders reported seeing it go bright pink. A fight ensued, and they fought in Trili's great hall. The books referred to this moment as the Fight of the Lions. Already greatly wounded, Trili fought hard. It ended with Pisne stabbing Trili in the heart."

Tommy went silent for a while. I'm sure it was tough for him to read all this and come up with a summary that a dumb fuck like me could understand. None of this shit made sense.

"The cleaver was so pleased with this sacrifice that it took Trili's entire body. The book said that it was 'sucked up.' Perhaps it's stored inside like a Narnia closet. I don't fucking know. Pisne, however, was drunk on power. After killing his brother, he claimed Trili's kingdom as his own and ordered almost everything to be sent back to his original kingdom. After a year, Yurt had heard of the story and the Battle of the Lions and visited Pisne. Pisne had created a kingdom of pure power where no one was free, and everyone worked long days fishing and shipping. His original kingdom became a world hub for buying and trading. He was powerful, rich, and mean. Yurt was appalled and ordered his army to squash Pisne.

"Pisne killed his army with a snap of his fingers. One book called it the 'First Wish.' Yurt was powerless, and all he had were plants. He brought Pisne an offering gift soon after he had sent the army. It was a pine tree, small but firm. Pisne laughed at his brother and the tiny tree he had brought. He picked up the cleaver and decapitated him before he even set foot in the kingdom walls." Tommy let out a long breath.

"What I'm trying to say, Justin, is that the founding king of all of this shit was corrupt as hell. They say that after he killed Yurt, his pinky turned purple. I don't know what that cleaver does, but it only brings bad news. I don't know why my finger is gold, but the colors stem from the kings and their offspring—our blood. After Pisne had killed his brothers, the offspring of both deceased kings suddenly had their pinkies missing. A chain reaction. They all turned the color of their fathers. Trili's children were blessed with pink nubs, and Yurt's children had green ones Killing someone with that cleaver seems to affect generations. But the gold, Gabby's final wish, and her having green can only mean one thing, Tin. Gabby is a life bringer, one of the purest offspring described in the book. She must be able to reincarnate so many times. That may have the most power."

I nodded on the other side of the phone. "A final wish. If this shit has been around for years, you would think we would have heard about some famous green pinky who solved world hunger or something. Or wished for enough money to solve it all, right?"

I tried to make the conversation light again. The money raining down from the ceiling was vivid in my head. In all this time, someone, somewhere, must have had enough to look suspicious. With these wishes being around for years, the news had barely covered anything. These Hand Bearers existed under the radar and stayed out of political power. I could only imagine that was Jeremi's next move.

"Only purple can wish for money, supposedly linked to the corruption of the King."

That's why Jeremi had been shocked. I took a second to absorb everything and get my thoughts straight. I just had one burning question for my brother.

"Well, what do you think is the strongest color?" I asked Tommy.

He was silent for a bit.

"Purple."

Then he hung up on me.

CHAPTER
TWENTY-SIX

I did not feel like I was the strongest person. I felt like I was the shittiest person.

My life was "wished" to be awful. I had no say in it. Just like Yurt had no say in his hand getting chopped off. Looking at Beth now, sleeping on the couch, I felt a deep sense of protectiveness and longing. She looked so peaceful as her body moved in time with her breathing. I imagined that I could see a future where she woke up and looked at me with those big green eyes. I could see the future that could have been. Although unsure what would happen with all this demon-and-devil stuff, Gabby and I would've been happy. We would have been happy even with Beth. I don't know why she never told me. She would have been an accident, just like Tommy was.

Mom got pregnant with Tommy in high school. When she was 17, she had no clue what she was doing, and I gave her credit for doing her best with all she had to deal with. Trying to figure out life with your high school sweetheart who begged you to get rid of the child must've been overwhelming. She stood her ground.

I'd give her that. I couldn't tell you why I was born. Probably another accident.

Beth's change into a black dress and her braided brown hair gave her a somber, Wednesday Addams–like vibe, emphasizing her mood and character.

"Make me something to eat; I'm hungry."

I had forgotten that I hadn't had anything to eat today besides the coffee Rose made. My stomach replied to her before I could.

"Make me chicken nuggets!" she yelled, and her eyes flashed blood red.

Before I knew what I was doing, I got up and entered the kitchen. My body walked around to each cabinet and grabbed the essentials for chicken nuggets. I had not been in this kitchen in at least a decade. Hell, I didn't even know this kitchen because Candace had remodeled everything. I was watching myself from a weird third-party point-of-view. I saw Rose from the corner of my eye with her mouth open. She was surprised that I knew where everything was and acted so robotically.

Beth scooted a stool to the kitchen's bar counter and awaited her chicken nuggets. She looked pleased with herself, folding her tiny hands over one another.

No wonder your parents didn't like you.

Fuck. I'm her parent. I'm her real dad. At least, I think so. But this commanding shit has got to stop. I think she got all of it from Gabby. The possessed Gabby.

After I made her chicken nuggets, I brought them over to her, and before I could set the plate down, she looked at me.

"Thanks, Daddy," she smiled at the end.

Maybe she's not so bad.

Once the plate was set down, I regained control of my body. I stepped back and stared at the little hand that started to poke a nugget.

"You can't do that again," I told her. "It's not very nice to make people do things they don't want to do."

"Monster Mommy didn't seem to mind," she said as she took a bite.

"Yeah, well, non-monster Daddy minds."

"I guess I could stop for Daddy."

I smirked as I thought I had just accomplished my first parenting task. This shit was hard. It felt like I was reading a book, but it was all gibberish.

I stole one of her nuggets and walked off.

"Daddy is going to be right back."

I walked over to the shelf where the bar was, where Candace had somehow opened the door to the basement of torture. The door had closed since the last time I was there, and I began looking for a key. I was looking at the dust on the shelf, and which bottles didn't have dust. I saw that a shot glass and a bottle of Crown were spotless. I gripped the bottle, and it moved towards me; I continued to push it down like a handle. Something clicked. We're getting there. I think she moved the shot glass, so I moved it to the right. Nothing clicked. I moved it to the left, and something clicked. A small finger scanner emerged from the space where the shot glass had been sitting.

Shit.

How could I get through this? I considered my options. Jeremi and Candace were gone, and there were no fingerprints there. I could find something in this godforsaken place that might still display a fingerprint, but I didn't feel like going on a treasure hunt.

I heard some footsteps behind me.

Rose stepped back from her trance, her eyebrows furrowing as she looked at me, confusion flickering across her face, revealing her surprise.

"Uh, well...Behind this wall is a weapon room. But Jeremi's uncle Lent is also kept down there. He's, like, frozen. It's weird, but I wanna ask him some questions."

"Oh...interesting," she said while her eyebrows furrowed together, somehow stuck between confusion and trying to understand how Lent was here.

"Yeah, I came here with Gabby before."

"Why?"

"She wanted to see what was up with Jeremi. The whole plan of coming here was probably to find Lent and the watch. But maybe it was to kill Jeremi. He wasn't home at first, but once he was, shit hit the fan."

"Shit hit the fan!" Beth echoed from the kitchen.

I shook my head and looked down.

"I need a fingerprint, though." I motioned to the little pad that popped up.

Rose looked at it briefly and immediately said, "Beth probably has access."

It dawned on me that these people were pretty fucked up

and were thinking of getting more swords for their kids 'cause it was 'safer.' Fucking Jeremi.

Speaking of the little devil, Beth seemed to pop up in between us.

"You guys wanna go into the playroom?"

Holy shit. The 'playroom'? Parenting this girl would be more challenging than I had imagined.

She touched the reader like a feather falling on the ground. The instant her finger hit the pad, a giant creak followed. We were in.

Just walking into the room was so fucking intimidating. It made Gabby's wall look so inferior. I wonder if she made the wish for the wall after her thing with Jeremi. Maybe seeing his impressive collection sparked some jealousy or want inside her.

Rose gasped under her breath as Beth ran out in front of us. Everything was the same as the last time I had been there. A pile of rubber ducks was still sitting there, and the blue glow from the small air duct was still present.

Beth picked up one of the small swords and swung it several times in front of her. The motions were fluid, and I was impressed.

Rose looked at her with a side glare. I felt like this was all weird to her. She was slowly taking everything in. I saw her eyes follow the wall to the taxidermied hands. She gasped and put her hands over her mouth.

"Are those...?"

"Wishing Hands? Yeah," I told her. I looked up and tried to read that stupid plaque again. Having all the fingers intact besides the nub. I caught the color of it. It was purple.

“Hey, Beth?”

“Yeah, Daddy?” she said as she swung again. “Gotcha!” she told the invisible man.

“Do you know whose hands those are?”

There were a couple more swings she had to get out before she said, “They’re Steven’s hands. Mr. Johnson. He worked with monster Dad.”

I felt the room shake. I had to sit down. Those were my father’s hands.

Chapter
Twenty-Seven

y father was a man who grew up wealthy. He didn't have to worry about much. Once my mom got pregnant, he was shunned by his family, therefore giving up any inheritance he was promised. I admired him for that when I first found out. I thought it was brave of him to choose love over wealth. The more I discovered over the years, the more I cut my reality in half. He had begged her to get rid of the baby.

He would always choose the money, and my mother would gain a large inheritance from her parents. Her father was already gone when she and my dad got together. My sneaky snake of a father was waiting for her mother to die. He probably played a hand in her death anyway, because she died just after Tommy was born.

Never getting a clear answer on how she died, I asked him one day. I think I was around fifteen. I was old enough to understand was what a natural cause of death and what wasn't. I should have just left the room once he smiled at me.

"Oh, Justin. Let me tell you something." He motioned for me to sit next to him on that awful-smelling velvet couch.

"When your mother got pregnant, we were struggling. By some gracious supernatural act, your grandmother was struck by lightning. She owned a farm, you see; she was out during a storm." The smile never left his face while describing all of this. "I believe it was a great power that was responsible." He winked and pointed upward.

I left right after that, back to my room. I felt like my father was a heartless man. He showed no remorse towards my mother, leaving him or even talking about her parents. That's when I knew for sure that my father was not a nice man at all. I could see it when he would get mad at Tommy or my mom, but this was different. Besides the part where he came into play, my family history was a joke to him.

Staring at those hands, I could only think of all the crimes he committed. All the times he slapped me and said I was strong because he made me so. Fucking bullshit. *Bullshit.*

I felt like I had come out of a daze. Staring at my hands while kneeling on the floor, I saw my wishes in front of me—potential, strength that wasn't his. I felt like it was almost my destiny to stop all of this.

My father never showed his hands too much or played ball with us. He was gone all day. By this point, I was convinced he wore a fake pinky or something. Maybe he made a gross wish on someone else's hand, wishing that we would never notice the missing phalange. He was a deceiving bastard.

The anger and rage I had towards my father were building, and I felt like I could no longer hold it in. I had to find Lent and figure out everything my father had done. I need to get revenge.

My heart also sunk at the thought that my revenge might include Gabby somehow—not in a good way.

I stood up. "Those are my father's hands."

Rose looked so surprised. She placed her hand on my shoulder in an 'I'm here for you' way.

Beth looked up and pondered for a moment.

"Hi, Grandpa." Her little voice sounded so sweet. I hoped she never wanted to meet him. "He's also here." She pointed to the spot where she was swinging her sword.

Fucking hell, she can see ghosts now?

This parenting thing was getting too much for me now.

"He says he's sorry."

"I don't want to hear it."

"He says you look good."

"Beth, I don't want to hear it."

"He says he's sorry about Grandma."

"Beth, I said I *don't* want to hear it!"

"He says—"

"BETH, SHUT UP!" I exploded, and immediately regretted it. The air was still in the room, and Beth stared at me. She didn't start crying; she stared at me with huge eyes. Just standing there.

"He says you're just like him."

And then it was my turn to cry. I didn't want to fucking scream, but I had to admit to myself that I did miss my dad. I never wanted to be like him. There were times when he hoisted me onto his shoulders during parades so I could see better. The one time he played catch with me. On one occasion, I saw him and Mom dancing in the living room by candlelight. And now, who knows, the bastard could be helpful.

I sighed and looked at Beth.

"I'm sorry I yelled at you, honey. I am just dealing with a lot. Can you ask my dad a question for me?

"He can hear you." That was all she said.

"Hey Dad...uh...I'm a Hand Bearer, as you can tell. I am getting involved in this crazy shit and have no idea what I'm doing or what to do. I would talk to Lent about this, 'cause he's in the other room. Did you have any advice, though?"

I couldn't believe I was talking to my father again. Who was dead.

For a long moment, it was silent. Beth nodded and took in the information my ghost father was spewing out. She turned on her small heels and ran up to me.

"He says that Lent is a good start. Mommy is very powerful, and she needs to be stopped. A mass reaping is about to happen....save your wishes, but use them to your advantage. He wishes us luck and can't stay," she said, surprisingly well for remembering what was whispered through the air.

"Oh well, thanks." I looked around, hoping to catch a glimpse of him or something.

Tell Tommy I'm sorry. I love you.

I heard it said near my ear. No hot breath or trick of the wind; the room was still. I could have just hoped so hard that I hallucinated it, but I decided to think that he said it. He was strong enough to pass through the shitty ghost barrier.

I turned to the small door I was about to crawl through.

"Well, I have to go talk to Lent."

Rose nodded and took Beth back out towards the house. I figured Rose had had enough for the day. I couldn't imagine being told over and over again that your daughter was too powerful and was a threat to those around her. A memory of Beth's red eyes flashed in my head. The apple may not have fallen too far from the tree.

CHAPTER TWENTY-EIGHT

inally, I was back in the room. Still glowing a soft blue, Lent was floating on his back, looking at the ceiling.

So you're back, he said in my head. *You have some of your father left.*

He slowly turned around so that we could look at each other. I was unsure what he meant by my father being 'left' on me, but I continued anyway.

"You knew my father. It seems pretty well. What the fuck were you guys trying to do?"

Well, you see, we were very focused on wealth. The housing market was shit. We were living penny to penny. You knew your mother; she wanted a fancy life with the roses, kids, and all the expenses. Our partners wanted that, too. We felt trapped.

"You guys could have found different jobs," I flat-out told him.

We were creators. We had an image of the world in mind and ways to thrive. We found the wishes and ran with them. The wishes could be used to our advantage, but we also hoped that someday, the world could use them to the people's advantage. It was your father who stopped us.

Of course, it was him. Just when I had finally let some of that anger resolve, it was biting my ass again.

He wanted more for himself. Jeremi agreed with him. They started having meetings of their own. Your father was... stubborn.

I could see that.

Why the fuck am I telling you this? What's in it for me?

By now, his body had turned around, and his unblinking eyes were staring at my forehead. I hated how his mouth didn't move, but I felt like I had to do something. He couldn't stay here forever.

"Uh, I don't know. What do you want?" I crossed my arms.

The girl.

"Gabby?"

Not anymore. I want a small one. Beth, I believe.

My face got hot. "Why the fuck do you want my daughter?"

Lent's eyebrows raised in a weird, slow way.

So you know?

"Yeah, I know."

I want your daughter because she has power. She is the spawn of hate. Her wishes are commands, and she has an unlimited number of them. She is a powerful demon. We finally created something worth it. I want to help her have a good life. She is such a strong girl. She gets it from her mother.

That last part was a jab at me. He was making me seem like a bottom feeder. I had contributed nothing to the making of Beth.

I was the last pick at the school dodgeball game. After all, I was a loser.

"Never."

I see you have become attached; that's too bad. She'll kill you then.

"No, she fucking won't." I had to say it out loud, so that I believed it, too. She couldn't, right?

We'll see about that. But if you don't give me the girl, I have no more information for you.

"What if I could get you out?" I looked around the room. I figured I could wish him out; purple is the most powerful color.

Tempting. I doubt you can. And even then, there is nothing in my life for me anymore. Your father ruined the company, and now Jeremi has fucked it over past the point of return. If you won't give me the girl, it's time for you to stop her—both of them.

"How?" I raised my hands towards the ceiling. This shit was getting ridiculous. I didn't know what I was doing. I didn't know if I could even stop Gabby in the first place. But also, did I have to stop Beth?

Make a wish.

He laughed. I could hear it outside of my mind. It was slow, just like his motions, and so very creepy.

"Fuck you." I left him there.

Walking back toward the kitchen, I reviewed everything I had learned. It wasn't much, but my father had been helpful in a way. A mass reaping was about to happen. Gabby was behind it, since he and Lent said she needed to be stopped. I was surprised she hadn't shown up herself. One thing was for sure, though: I had to stop her.

It clicked.

She was probably out making more Hand Bearers.

I went into the kitchen and told Rose everything. Beth was also in the room, but I figured she was a part of it as much as I was. She was being targeted, too. I knew Lent wanted her, but now I didn't know who else did.

"I can find Mommy." Beth peeped out at the end of the spiral of information I tossed at them.

Rose and I looked dumbfounded.

"How?"

Her eyes closed, and she focused on her breath for a moment. When she opened them, they were deep red, and her hair started floating around her a bit.

"Where is Gabriella Nunez?" The layered voices were coming out of her this time. They sounded different from Gabby's voice but were still nails on a chalkboard. Maybe she was the Antichrist or some shit. Her little hands were in the air, acting like a compass. Eventually, her right index finger pointed towards the west.

"I see her. She's by Avondale." Beth's voice was still not her own. "Go find her, Justin."

I looked at Rose, and she nodded a little. "I'll go with you."

I didn't know what to do with Beth. She was so small and could probably not hold herself in a fight; I didn't want her to get hurt. As if she was reading my mind, she returned to her young childish voice and said, "I'm fucking coming with you."

"Then let's fucking go" was all I could say back to her.

We all agreed that weapons would be good, and since we had access to so many, we returned to the weapon room. I grabbed a small sword like the one from Gabby that had disappeared somewhere between getting knocked out and waking up. I also grabbed a pistol identical to the one I had given Tommy, which fit nicely in the small of my back. Unsure what to do with the weapons since I couldn't hold anything, I figured it was better to be safe than sorry. Rose grabbed what looked like a steel bat with nails poking out of it—apocalyptic style. I nodded and gave her a thumbs-up.

But Beth was on a mission. She went to one of the walls and punched in some code.

"This is where I keep *my* toys," she giggled. The wall gave way to another small room. It was decked out in rainbows and weapons of all kinds. She bounced over to a portion of the room and grabbed two stuffed animals. One was a bat, just like the last one I saw her with, and the other was a teddy bear. How the *fuck* was she going to be helpful with those? I was beginning to have my doubts about her. She came out of the room beaming and held them up.

"Nice," I said. "Are you going to beat Mom to death with fluff?"

It felt weird calling Gabby "Mom." I kept reminding myself that I had to detach. I had to become this role model now, and we didn't have space or time to figure out how a devil would fit within that mix.

Beth rolled her tiny eyes and left me with a cliffhanger. "You'll see."

Looking around, I did a mental inventory. I felt like I was going off to war. If only Tommy had been there, I'd have felt more confident leading everyone out of the house. My team of misfits was ready, though. Before we left the room, an intrusive thought, 'Take some wishes,' came to mind, and we were surrounded by those hands again. Part of me wanted to take my father's hands. I concluded that they were all cursed and that I needed all the good luck I could get.

We all headed towards the door and stepped outside. I turned around and considered what I was about to do. There would be no harm, and I could create a haven, if anything. I looked at the door.

"I wish only Rose, Beth, and I can enter this house."

My left hand lifted, and time froze. Suddenly, the door opened, and my hand was shoved into the frame. In one swift motion, the door slammed shut on my right index finger and popped it off—another one down, only two more to go.

It was a lovely day, and the blue sky was around us. It felt like a good day to die.

CHAPTER TWENTY-NINE

I was angry with Gabby. Frustrated with her and her choices. How could she have done all of this? I had a kid, and she didn't tell me. She probably never would have. Now, she was the vessel for Satan and was hunting me down. Hell, she turned my brother into a demon. She was selfish and sealed the deal by finding me to get me involved. I was furious.

We made our way towards Avondale. It was on a strip with many other restaurants and bars. It seemed busy; I guessed it was a Friday night. I'd gotten to the point in this adventure where I didn't even know the fucking day. Great.

Beth was playing with the stuffed animals, making them walk along the sidewalk lines while giving them little voices. It was cute. I would have enjoyed this time together more if we hadn't been trying to track down Gabby. Unsure what would happen when we got there, I slowed down. I looked over at Rose and whispered under my breath to her, "I don't know a damn thing I'm doing."

"You're doing great. We can try to talk to Gabby when we find her. I know she doesn't want to hurt you, and I'm sure she doesn't want to hurt Beth," she said with a half-smile. "I don't know about myself, though."

"Have you seen Duckie recently?" I asked. I felt rude for not asking before.

"No, sadly." She looked down. "Gabby told him I was dead."

Gabby and Rose had always had a rocky relationship. Rose seemed like she'd calmed down a bit, but when Gabby's dad was around, things got even weirder. I didn't know much, but Gabby and Duckie were from their dad's previous marriage. He met Rose and dumped the kids on her. Their biological mother had been out of the picture since Duckie was born. Their dad tried, but something in him broke. Given the weird situation, Rose took them in and tried to make a home for them. Of course, feeling like they didn't belong, Gabby started acting out, prompting Rose to go into protection mode. Looking at Beth, I could see how that would happen. Gabby had dumped her on Jeremi and Candace.

Longing for her dad, though, Gabby never really gave Rose a chance. She always summed it up as 'She's crazy' or 'She lost half her brain again.' Now, I felt so thankful that I had run into Rose and sympathized with her.

"That's fucked up," I told her.

"Yeah, well, kids have their minds," she said.

When we got to Avondale, we stopped and went inside. There was a section for restaurant dining, so we sat down and ordered some food. The benches were bright red, and the table was still sticky from the previous diners.

"What will you do with the rest of your wishes?" Rose asked me.

I looked down and thought for a second.

"I have no idea. Step one is to figure out what's up with Gabby, right?" I felt like I was asking the air to tell me the answer. Whisper the secret code for what to do next. God, I wished Tommy had found a guidebook or some shit.

"I think I'll get a new house," Rose said.

"I'd wish for a bat." Beth chimed in. Her little grin of shark teeth beamed at me.

It was nice hearing what the future could hold. Part of me thought I'd never see the day Beth got her bat.

So, fuck it.

"I wish for a bat for Beth," I decided.

My dumbass did this in the middle of a restaurant. My hand was on the table. The dull butter knife or whatever sad excuse of a knife the restaurant gave you slid across the table by itself and lifted to cut my left thumb off. It seemed to have some trouble as it started sawing back and forth. For a second, I thought it would never end. When time returned, the knife had lost its life, and there was no blood on the table.

A bat appeared, and Beth gasped. Then I registered what had just happened.

I wished for a fucking *bat* in the middle of a *restaurant*.

Chaos erupted as the bat started flying all over the place. It didn't have a leash, or anything attached to it, so once someone opened the door, it flew out. Then chaos erupted at our table as Beth started wailing.

Great, I fucked up. Damn, waste of a wish.

I wanted to think my fatherly instinct made me wish for the

bat. Although short-lived, I hoped the gesture showed Beth that I cared about her. I had never known she existed, but now that I did, I wanted to be a role model for her. I also wanted to be better than my father. Rose was giving me a death stare.

"You idiot," she said under her breath through gritted teeth.

We got kicked out of Avondale and were on the road again. We debated where to go next and decided to return to the house. We turned the corner to go, and there she was. Gabby.

I checked really quick in my head. I took inventory and tried to make a battle plan. We still had weapons, and I could feel the pistol and the knife on me. Rose seemed tense, and Beth could have cared less about Gabby standing there. She let out a little sniffle from crying about the bat.

"Look at that," Gabby yelled. "My big happy family is all together."

Her arms opened up like she wanted to give us all a hug. She was back in her leather gear. Head to toe, all in black. Her dark hair was framed around her face, and the wind blew slightly. I was surprised she didn't kill us right away. Or did she even want to kill us? I was all sorts of confused.

"Nice to see you again, Gabby, "I said and waved. God, she looked beautiful.

Rose punched me in the shoulder. We were leaving friendliness behind. Why was I such a sucker for her?

"What do you want?" Gabby asked.

I was unsure how to answer because I didn't know what I wanted. I wanted all this shit to be back to normal. I looked at Rose.

"Gabby, what do you want?" Rose fired back at her. She crossed her arms as if she were her mom again. Scolding her for sneaking out again.

Gabby seemed taken aback by the question. She lowered her arms and shook her head. Her body posture seemed to change a bit, but she still looked like herself, and for a second, I felt as though there was no evil present. A thread tugged at one of her eyebrows. She turned around with her back facing us.

"I guess what I want," she started, "is for you to leave me the fuck alone."

She turned around and started walking off.

In my head, I thought this would be like a movie. She could fly at us and spew fire—the epic fight scene. Or blow up a building again, like when she found the cleaver. I was prepared to shoot her, goddamn. I was confused. But also, I felt relieved. I watched her walk away from us, eager to chase after her.

Tommy and Lent's voices echoed in my head: *She's getting stronger; you must stop her*. That was what I had to do.

Until I realized I couldn't move.

Gabby had spread her arms out enough that her sleeve lifted a little. I saw the gold glimmer flash on her wrist. She had stopped us cold in our tracks.

When she turned around, the cleaver was in her mouth. Her eyes went back to the empty black.

Rose and Beth also realized they couldn't move, and Beth started to whimper.

When Gabby pulled the knife out of her mouth, she did it slowly, and she licked it, letting her snake-like tongue flick back and forth on the sharp edge. I thought that was fucking disgusting.

"I guess I do want something, Mom." She slowly walked towards us, knowing she was in control of our bodies. The street-lamp offered a little light, revealing that her hair was beginning to shift color. The shadow she cast in the light was barely there. Her footsteps were heavy and purposeful. She wasn't here to play house. "I would love to have your wishes."

Saying 'wishes' was the trigger for her layered voices. The word echoed around us, and the delayed demon voices came out. I was now convinced that the Gabby I had spent time with was never the real one. She was way too far gone. She was just really good at masking it. But now that we knew, why would she mask it? I had to think of something fast. I couldn't move. Gabby was getting closer. I saw something move out of the corner of my eye. It was a bat.

A fucking bat.

Chapter Thirty

I guess I'd always wondered how I would die. When I was younger, I thought it would be at my father's hands. Or the school bully. Maybe Jeremi would go crazy one day, and the beatings he gave me might be fatal. When I played baseball, I would think that one super-fast pitch or ball coming at me could hit me in the head, and then I would be as good as dead. For ballet, I imagined falling off the stage and hitting my head against a seat. Recently, it was freezing my balls off so badly in New Mexico that I would turn into a human popsicle and never wake up. I guess I'd never been afraid of it. But now I was scared of dying at the hands of my devil ex-girlfriend. Beth had a different idea.

The bat swooped down and hit Gabby in the face. I thought it was hilarious, but I couldn't laugh.

She started waving her arms around frantically and swinging the cleaver in the air, hoping to cut it. Beth's stuffed animals were on the sidewalk. One was on each side of her as she had dropped them to the ground. The bat started to move, and so did the bear. They seemed to be slowly coming to life, changing and growing into real, life-sized animals. Beth was fucking awesome.

While Gabby was still preoccupied, the bear that had grown into a full-sized grizzly bear was marching towards her. The other bat started hitting Gabby's head and grabbing her hair. It was about twice the size of the bat that I had wished for. With one full swing, the bear put Gabby to the ground. She was out cold from hitting her head.

We could move again, and I rushed over to grab Gabby's watch.

Once I moved her sleeve, I could see something that would change things. The watch was shattered. The face sported a new array of broken glass, and its shimmer seemed gone. The bear stood there waiting for commands, and the bats stopped. I looked back, and they were both perched on Beth's shoulders.

"Good pets" was all she said. The devilish grin plastered across her face.

I saw Rose grabbing the cleaver off the ground from the corner of my eye. Fuck yeah.

I stood over Gabby and waited for her to say something. Her face started to become disorientated. Her beautiful alabaster skin had some blood on it from the bat pulling out her hair. She blinked hard and opened her eyes wide to look at me. I was taken by surprise and stepped one step back.

"You stupid idiots. I was going to save the world," she spat out some blood from her mouth. It landed with a splat next to her face. "Don't you like your wishes? You can wish your life didn't suck, Justin. Just fucking reverse it. Why are you being so awful?"

Her voice was back to normal, and it was hard not to help her. Or brush her hair out of her face.

I heard the grunt before I saw the kick.

Rose was now standing next to me and had kicked Gabby on her ribs.

"You would kill your whole fucking family? With no remorse? What kind of *monster* are you?" Rose yelled at her. She gave her another slight kick.

Gabby curled up in a fetal position and was quiet for a second. Then she started making a noise that sounded like crying for a bit, but I realized she was laughing as it got louder.

"Gabby, what the fuck?" I asked the empty shell of a human. Her face snapped toward me.

"I'm your worst nightmare." She said it slowly, and her tongue flicked out of her mouth. It was pointed like a snake. The dark, blood-red stain started to spread across her body. She could've been an art piece if her body had begun turning human flesh to this deep red. All I knew was that I had to get the fuck out of there. Now.

I turned and grabbed Beth's small hand in mine. I motioned to Rose to turn around and *run*.

Shit, shit, shit.

I didn't feel prepared. I knew we had weapons, but we needed to return when I had learned how to solve all this. Everyone had told me that I was powerful, yet I couldn't even stand to face her right now. I heard something happening behind me, and I made the mistake of taking a peek. She was entirely off the ground, and her air was glowing, pointed towards the sky. She looked like how she was when Jeremi met his eventual end.

"You just can't run *away*," Gabby yelled at us.

I suddenly stopped. What the fuck was running going to do? This was probably my only time to shine.

"Hey, Gabby," I let go of Beth's hand and stepped towards the tornado of a woman, "Do you remember when you first met me?"

The question did not faze her, so I continued. She was moving her hands like she was conjuring something.

"I was sitting right over there." I pointed to the sidewalk on my way to my house. "I was crying."

She hadn't said anything or moved, which was a good sign. Then, a bunch of knives appeared next to her right hand. Floating around in a circle, they glinted angrily when they caught the light from the post, waiting for her command to pierce me like a good piece of steak. But I continued.

"My dad had just given me his opinion about my wanting to join the ballet club. I was bleeding, and you brought me a towel. You said something that has stuck with me ever since—do you remember that, Gabby?"

She blinked and looked down at me.

Her eyes were that dark black, with no green visible.

"We were only ten, but you said the most profound shit." I smiled up at her. I had the overwhelming feeling that I still loved her. So much.

She blinked again, and I saw her eyes turn back to green this time. Striking against the deep red of her skin, I could see it from the ground.

"Never let an asshole tell you what to do," she said in a normal voice. The knives dropped onto the sidewalk. Just as soon as I noticed it was only her voice saying it, not the layers, it hurt my heart. She was still there.

Her eyes turned back to black.

"Nice one, Justin," the layered voices told me. "You got her back for just a second. Too bad she isn't strong enough to fight me. Let's see if *you* are."

In one swift motion, I was on my back, gasping for air. The beast in the vessel had pressed her way down and pushed me hard onto the floor. It was hard to recollect myself, but I knew I had to protect Beth. And Rose. And Gabby. Fucking hell.

I could see for a second and wondered where all the normal people were. Weren't they seeing this? Was this not on the news?

The darkness was engulfing us. The sun wouldn't rise for at least another six hours. I knew I had to act fast, as we would have the most cover in the darkness. I saw Rose lunge at Gabby when she got close again. Her steel bat swung back and forth like a shield around her. Beth was curled beneath her bear, who growled and protected her. The bats were perched on the bear's head and ready to fight. I needed to get off my ass.

What did it even mean if I were the strongest of the 'colors' here? What could I even do? Why the fuck did Gabby want the wishes so badly? I suddenly remembered that Rose had something.

"I need the cleaver!" I yelled at her. I started to get up and was poised on one knee, kneeling. The air around us was getting cold, and debris was flying in the whirlwind wherever Gabby went.

I felt like a giant mosquito was attacking me.

Gotta squish her somehow. Trap her.

Rose looked up from whatever she was swinging at and took the cleaver out of her waistband. She threw it at me.

Aw fuck, you've got to be kidding me.

I said a few swear words I hoped Beth didn't hear and ran towards the cleaver. I had no idea how to catch it, given that I only had two fingers. I tapped into my old baseball skills and started sliding toward it. As it was coming down, I completely missed it, and the blade fell perfectly right on top of my left middle finger. Sliced it.

Shit.

CHAPTER THIRTY-ONE

I was in pain. It was excruciating. My whole body felt on fire, and I couldn't escape. I was standing in a space I was unfamiliar with. I squinted, trying to open my eyes. It was so bright. Before me, it was all white. I looked at my hands and had all my fingers again, except for the pinky that got cut off. It felt like someone had ripped away the scenery, leaving me all alone in the vast, open white space.

I took a step forward, not knowing where I would go, but I felt like I had to return to the fight. I had to protect them. What a fuck up I was.

When I turned around, I got a good surprise.

Sitting in a giant red velvet chair with his legs crossed and lips around a pipe, it was my good friend, Lent.

"What the fuck are you doing here?" I asked him. My voice echoed like we were in a deep cave.

"Nice of you to finally join me," he put the pipe down, "I see Gabby finally got you."

"No," I thought, thinking of how I had ended up here. "I mean, yeah, it seems like it."

“Welcome to the abyss.” He motioned his hands around him like he was showing off a new house. “I got sent here by Jeremi.”

“But I talked to you; your body is in the real world,” I told him, “Right?”

He smirked at me.

“You dumbass, can’t you see? This is purgatory. You’re dying slowly, just like I am in that forbidden jello. I could talk to you because *you* have the power to go in between.”

“What the hell do you mean by that?” I crossed my arms. Suddenly, I felt all my fingers. It was so weird to have them all again. “What the *fuck?*”

“Poor kid doesn’t even know his power yet,” Lent commented, like he was talking to a live audience. I wanted to punch this guy so badly.

He got up from his chair and started to walk towards me. I was hesitant and unsure whether he was a friend or a foe, but I had nowhere else to go, so I stayed put.

“Your power comes from that color on your pinky. It took a lot of trial and error to find what is strongest and who might possess it. I’m sure you’ve heard of the experiments.”

“Yeah, Gabby told me about them. I mean, some of them.”

“She probably told you the cleaver doesn’t do anything. If anything, it drives people insane. Because those people are not like us. We’re *special.*”

He started to pace around me. Circling me like a vulture. Just like Gabby did at Jemeri’s house in the grass.

I thought about what Tommy said about the kings and how purple came from the corrupt king. I was not going to reveal to

Lent that I knew this information, as I thought it could give me an upper hand later in this weird-ass conversation.

"Green and purple go hand in hand. Life and death. Light and darkness. Do you get what I'm saying?"

"I was told that the last wish has the power of life and death. That's why Gabby is the way she is; she wished for Tommy to return to life."

"Oh, your poor brother. That was a mistake that shouldn't have happened. You're almost correct." He chuckled a bit. "If only your father could see you now."

He took a big puff of his pipe and blew out the brightest yellow smoke. I couldn't smell anything and wondered what the hell was in it. It didn't smell like anything, either.

"Lent, can you just tell me what's going on?" I felt defeated, but I wanted to get back.

"I told you, you're in purgatory. We are stuck here in the realm where we neither live nor die. The cleaver, because you are a Royal Hand Bearer, didn't drive you insane or instantly kill you. It sent you here. You have royal blood. Also, that's why Tommy didn't die when Gabby used the cleaver after his little revival. Our poor girl Gabby has lived so many lives because she is green, meaning eternal life. She was the perfect test subject until the baby was born. She kept that as a great secret, eh?" he laughed. "But right now, her body is different because of all the experiments." She's lived so many lives that they all blur into one. She's on her tenth revival. The cleaver favored her. Long ago, it was said that the royal ones carried the cleaver around and could escape from physical form at will. The greatest wish. This allowed their bodies to die while their souls carried on. Perhaps transferred to a different vessel. Great for wars."

I thought about how Pisne had killed his brothers. Were they sent to this place? Were all the sacrifices sent here, too? I looked around the empty room. Lent said only the Royal ones could be here. At that moment, it was just him and me. Where the fuck was everyone else? There had to be some lost souls here that never made it back to the physical realm.

I could only imagine what was happening to my body in the real world. Had Gabby already ripped me in half?

"How can I get back to my body?" I asked, feeling awful that he would say it was impossible.

"Why would you want to?"

"I sure as hell don't want to be stuck in this shithole with you," I told him, looking around at all the white open space. "Also, where the fuck is everyone else if they could escape their physical form?"

He laughed, and it sounded like a broken music box.

"They're all dead!" He laughed and made a motion as if he had his head cut off. He continued, "Of course, I hunted the Royal Blood first. Special cases like Gabby and us are the only ones left."

"What about the ancient ones? Like Yurt?"

His face changed into surprise. He wasn't expecting me to know that.

"So you know the whole back story now, do you?" He raised an eyebrow and pushed back the strand of hair that had fallen into his face. "I also took care of them. It had been so long for their souls that Jeremi and I came here before he betrayed me. I showed him the true, full power he could have. When we got here, we banished their souls with the curse."

He could see my puzzled expression after he said that.

"The curse. The curse of never having peace, never getting to rest. We banished them to hell." He lifted his chin. He was proud.

Tommy never said anything about a curse. Hell, he never said anything about an endless white purgatory that waited for the souls of the Royal Hand Bearers. I had no hope in Lent anymore. This guy was evil.

"What happened to Gabby's soul?" I looked around, searching for it. Please tell me he didn't banish her, too.

"Gabby has gone through possession, Justin. She's unable to go back to her human form. Her physical form has to be killed off, and then maybe her soul can return to the world." He snapped with his right two fingers, and a white wall started moving towards us.

Behind the wall, once it moved off to the right, was a figure resembling Gabby, except she was glowing white. Not in the fiery 'I'm going to kill you' way, but in a soft, angelic way, like mist.

"Gabby!" I ran over to her. She was curled up, holding her legs against her chest, and her expression was pretty blank. She was dressed in white from head to toe, and her hair was dark gray.

"It took a lot out of her. I remember when Jeremi pressured her into the experiments. Too bad she didn't want to be strong. Who knew she'd be the perfect match?"

"Perfect match for what?" I was getting sick of him circling this conversation.

"Lucifer."

He had confirmed for sure what Tommy had thought. I had been going around for multiple days with the *devil.* I held hands with it. Was she the devil the whole time?

Holy shit, I need to cleanse myself.

How can I save her now?

My brain was starting to give up hope fast.

"I told you she was powerful, especially since she has a little bit of my blood coursing through her veins. It was another failed experiment," Lent smirked with every comment he made. I thought he didn't want to help and was fine being in his jello forever. But he wanted me to suffer at the hands of his knowledge.

"I'm going to destroy Lucifer, then."

This time, the broken music box laugh echoed loudly.

"Boy, you don't even know your power. Green and purple are the strongest colors because they complement each other. You are death; she is life."

"What the fuck does that mean?"

A split-second thought ran through my head. Is that how Candace wished for the baby, if she could wish for life? She must've harvested another green hand from a relative of Gabby's.

"How many wishes do you have left, in physical form?" Lent asked.

"I have one."

I recalled the knife flying and cutting my finger in half.

"Maybe half of one." I corrected myself.

"Half should still work, but I have never tried to wish off a half of a finger," he seemed intrigued. Since you are a Royal, you have an extra life-or-death wish. For her, it is life; for you, it is death. You can wish for either with the last wish, since you are purple, but not many people know you get an extra one. You could have used yours, but you can choose with just one left—life or death."

"What about you? What the fuck does pink mean?" I stared at his pinky nub. It was that hot pink I had only seen on Jeremi before. That meant that he came from the bloodline of Trili, and Tommy never said what his kingdom was known for. Life, death, and what. Love?

"Resurrection." Lent bluntly said, with his eyes glaring at me.

"How the fuck is that different than life? Doesn't that mean you can bring people back to life?"

"True, not very different, but it makes all the difference. The green of life can bring people back to life, but not fully. I can, however, bring people back even if they've passed on to heaven or hell. I am the bringer of the rest to the unrest. Chaos, if you will. I came from the kingdom of war and fighting. Trili was a great leader and planned to overthrow his brothers before Pisne even had the chance. The cleaver fucked everything up. It would have been a beautiful domination." He grinned and stroked his hair again.

"So why didn't you wish for my father to come back? Or Jeremi?"

"The pink is also blessed with no sympathy or empathy. To only gain power for oneself. Resurrect the true warriors to continue the battle for you. Those two were just pawns."

I was convinced he had just referenced Jeremi and my father as objects, but I was not the one to defend them, either.

Those were the two men I hated most.

CHAPTER THIRTY-TWO

I recalled the cleaver being named 'warrior' and thought for a second that was one of the things Lent was hoping to resurrect. However, he already had it, so who else would he call upon?

"I was planning on resurrecting Trili himself." He crossed his arms. That was his plan? What about Gabby and Lucifer? He was already the most evil and powerful being. "Jeremi stopped me and placed me here. Very nice of him."

"What would that have done?" I couldn't stop my curiosity.

He smiled at me, and I wanted to look away. Sitting upright, he flung the pipe off to the right.

"Trili was the rightful owner of the cleaver. It never should have been Pisne. Trili could have resurrected all of the previous fallen soldiers and invaded the world. We could have dominated the whole globe together. Instead, lousy Pisne found it, and now we are here. The devil was only my plan to distract everyone else, especially Jeremi. I planned to control Lucifer as well. But he found out too soon and wanted it all to himself. We were so close."

I turned away. I couldn't believe this. Lent had used so many people to get his way, but it never turned out how he wanted. Now, he let loose Satan on the world and couldn't care less. Chaos? It's more like the destruction of the whole world.

"How do I save Gabby?"

"You can't." His wicked grin grew as he slowly stood up. "Not here. You need to return to the real world and figure out how to stop Lucifer. Gabby got here because of your brother."

"What?"

Lent sighed. He was getting just as annoyed with me asking questions as he was answering them.

"When she made the wish for Tommy to come back to life, she traded her soul instead of dying. The last bit of it that she had. She had so much hope in her. The purity of the wish and her love for you made the perfect vessel for it to take over. We had waited so many years. Jeremi and I had been keeping tabs on her. Despite his bullying, we couldn't get you away from her. When you left, we made a plan. We made her a Hand Bearer, but she didn't know. The trick of the golden watch," he winked. "Jeremi froze time one day when she was walking past, cut her finger, and wished for it to be disguised. No one knew but us. When Tommy got hit, she came to us crying and sobbing, knowing that we had a way to grant more substantial wishes. This was what we were waiting for. The breaking point. Poor girl. Along with the experiments with the cleaver, some evil spirits were already in her. The trade went seamlessly. She fought it for a long time, but as you can see now, she has given up."

At that moment, I felt I knew who was driving the truck that hit Tommy. He was standing in front of me.

"What the hell were you hoping to achieve by unleashing the devil?"

"Power."

I wanted to punch this guy so bad. So I did. Clocked him with a right uppercut straight to his chin.

Taken aback and holding his face, Lent retreated near Gabby's soul.

"Fuck you. I bet my dad was in on all of this, too." An image of him standing next to Tommy's casket entered my mind. He never cried that day. It made me think he knew that Tommy, indeed, wasn't dead, but also my father was that heartless as well.

Still holding his face but now looking like a scared deer in the headlights, he finally said what I wanted to hear. "He was. He was a Royal Bearer, just like you. He never used any of his wishes for himself. Other hand-bearers always make wishes for him. The sacrifices he made..."

"You mean the ones he killed?"

Lent frowned.

"He had to do it. This is a movement, Justin. A whole new generation. Anything at your fingertips."

"While innocent people get *killed*? I don't think so."

"It took us forever to find the objects. It was for the *benefit* of the people."

I thought about it for a second.

"You said you *found* the objects? Gabby said it was a family heirloom. The watch, at least. She didn't tell me where the cleaver was from."

He laughed at me. His fear was gone, as this realm didn't allow for pain. Lent just laughed with his whole body.

"Oh, what an oblivious loser you are. When your dad and I first thought of this, we had heard stories from our families. We had read about it in a book after my great-grandfather died. We were inspired." He gestured as if he had just had a brilliant idea. "The watch was an heirloom, but the battery is made from a stone found very far underground in the homeland. It's a kind of quartz but must be infused with Royal Bearer blood. That one took forever to figure out."

He saw me looking at him with disbelief.

"The one that Gabby has is the one your father had."

I pictured the broken watch face. I could feel my anger—inside me and out—almost like I had created an angry bubble that was ready to burst.

"And the cleaver?" I asked him, fuming.

He smiled, his teeth yellowing like the smoke he had blown out. "I asked for it."

"What the fuck does that mean?"

He walked around his chair while explaining his proud achievement of obtaining this cursed cleaver. Twenty years ago, he sacrificed a goat and his firstborn son.

I was speechless.

"I laid out two normal kitchen knives. I had obtained a book at the time with ancient spells. One was tied to the cleaver. You pray to the fallen angel; if you hadn't guessed by now, it's Lucifer." He sighed. "I put a drop of my blood on it at first, and then the sacrifices were made. I had to cut off all of my son's fingers and then behead the goat…"

"You sacrificed your *son*. Do you know how fucked up that is?"

"He lived—" Lent seemed taken aback, like he hadn't done anything wrong— "just like those stories in the Bible. It wasn't about the sacrifice but the trust and commitment to doing what had to be done. I just needed his fingers. The joining was completed after that. His fingers were granted back to him."

Harley came to my mind. He was trying to cut off my finger for Gabby. She said he had taken something from her for a very brief moment. I wondered if he had been trying to make a new cleaver with the weird dagger he had presented. I could feel my face get hot.

"Then the experiments happened with each item. The first business your father and I had together. Creating a Hand Bearer wasn't successful until two years ago. That's when the ball started rolling."

There was a weird sparkle in his eye. I pictured Jeremi, young and afraid, in his father's kitchen. My father was probably close by. It was apparent that Jeremi knew everything from the start and had tricked Gabby into thinking he knew nothing and was a good guy at first, all to gain her trust and make her the perfect vessel. I wanted to go back and never let this happen, but I couldn't.

I was done listening to the twisted ways Lent founded his new business. It made me sick to my stomach to think that my family was involved in this, that Gabby was engaged in this by force. I walked over to where she was, knelt, and looked at Gabby.

"Hey," I started talking to her, "Do you remember the first time we met?"

She blinked.

"She's not here, Justin. She's gone. Taken over. She can never return to her body."

I ignored what he was telling me.

"I know you wished for my life to suck, and I know that I messed everything up. For the whole time we've been apart, all I've been thinking about is you. I met Beth, and she's wonderful. A little weird, but wonderful." I started to reach out to her, wondering if I could touch her shoulder.

"Oh, you mean the devil child?" Lent said and rolled his eyes. "Another great, powerful being was a mistake, but hopefully we can get her back into the right hands. She is the offspring of a Royal Bearer and a demon vessel. She needs to be raised where she can express her true powers."

I kept ignoring him. My hand touched Gabby's shoulder gently. It felt like cold water, with a bit of tension, but it passed quickly, and her shoulder re-formed. I knew she must be in there somewhere.

"We can finally live at my old house and have a little happy family. Gabby, I know you're in there and I need your help. I need you to wake up. You have to protect our family."

Gabby blinked, and her eyes slowly met mine. Her eyes were a muted color from what I was used to seeing. In all honesty, she looked dead.

"Gabby," I deeply breathed, "I love you."

Lent burst out laughing—the tune of the broken music box

echoing off the walls again. I was the joke of the century for him. I didn't care at the moment. I was hoping that some honesty could unravel this whole thing. Not breaking eye contact, it almost looked like she was trying to get out of chains around her. Her body moved sharply and awkwardly. The movement caught Lent off guard, and he abruptly stopped laughing.

"This is fucking impossible" was all he managed to get out before Gabby was standing up.

She opened her mouth, but no sounds came out. She tried again and again: mouth open, then shut, open, then shut.

I looked down at my fingers and had no idea if it would work, but I gave it a shot. After all, I had powers, didn't I? I was stronger than Lent. Stronger than my father. Fuck it, I was stronger than Lucifer. I finally believed it.

"I wish Gabby could talk."

In this empty place, nothing appeared to take my finger away. It glowed a misty white—like Gabby was—and started to dissolve into the blank space.

"Don't let some asshole tell you what to do" were the first words out of her mouth. It was raspy, but it was her.

I hugged her. She was warm, no longer cold water, still glowing, a little transparent, but she was here. I felt like I had just finished a performance. The weight of relief was small but worth it.

"I still can't return to my body," she whispered.

"Why not?" I looked at her. I was so confused; this was all too much. I grabbed her shoulders to look at her face, only for her to turn away.

"I told you," Lent said, rolling his eyes, "you have to destroy her physical form. Lucifer controls it now."

"But then she'll have nobody to go to," I fired back.

"What do you think your daughter's stuffed animals are?"

Holy fucking shit.

"Those are...people?"

"Of course. Beth has the unique ability to come here, too. She harbored some of the people I had gotten rid of. She became attached, since I had to lure them to my home. Guess she has some form of a heart."

I felt like I was going to puke. What the hell was happening?

"Grab another stuffed animal and boom—you have your sweet Gabby back." At this point, Lent was just making fun of me.

"There has to be another way."

"Well, there is, but you're stuck here," he said, and plopped his happy ass back on the giant velvet chair.

"Can I stop it?"

"You have the extra wish," Gabby said. "Just kill me off."

"Gabby, this isn't just like killing off a character in a show," I said, also realizing it had been a long time since I sat down and watched TV.

"I'd rather be dead than have Lucifer keep my body for who knows how long," she said sadly.

"How the fuck would I even get back to do that?"

I looked down at my hands. The wishes have to do something. Lent said it was possible. The trick was believing I could make it happen. How stupid was this? I remembered watching *Peter Pan* with Duckie. Fairies only exist if you believe; maybe this fucked up wishing was the same. I couldn't think straight anymore, but my heart started racing, and I could feel myself getting hot from the adrenaline in my veins. I was from the bloodline of the corrupted king, so I had some devil in me, too, right?

"I got it."

I wished as I had never wished before. I wished for puppies, a cell phone, to be bald, a hat, a birthday cake, and a peach. One by one, they all appeared. One by one, my fingers dissolved into thin air. I had two wishes left. Before hearing anyone say anything to me, I looked up and hoped it wouldn't be the last time I saw Gabby. Her face was contorted in a way that I didn't understand.

"I wish for my soul to die here and be returned to my body."

I could hear Lent laughing again, and everything went black.

CHAPTER
THIRTY-THREE

hen my eyes finally opened, I was on my back, staring up at the stars. It was pretty; I could see the North Star. I couldn't hear anything besides the ringing in my ears. Suddenly, Beth's face was so close to mine that she was screaming at me, and tears fell down her face onto mine.

I gotta get up.

Finally returning to my usual self, I tried to stand up while hearing Beth screaming at me.

"She got Rose! Rose is dead!"

I felt like I was in that white room—nothing around me. I couldn't make sense of anything. Darkness. War zone.

I saw Rose's body lying flat near where I was lying on the asphalt, and I looked up to see the monster over me. Lucifer in Gabby's body had turned her skin a deep, dark red, but now there were black veins. Gone was all the leather that had covered her, leaving only her torn T-shirt and jeans. Her hair was glowing like white fire but looked like real fire. Her eyes were the same empty black, and as she spun in the air, the tornado of power around her followed. Small lightning bolts flashed, and I heard a boom of thunder. I thought of my mother's mom being killed by a random lightning bolt.

"How nice of you to join us, *Albert*." Lucifer's layered voices rang clear to me. He was teasing me.

I hadn't been called that name in so long, so it was weird to hear it again. I felt like Albert had died in this, and I was Justin again. I started to get up from where I was lying. I was shaky, but one leg straightened, and the other followed. I was going through my revival.

I looked down. Half of my middle finger remained. The cleaver stuck in the asphalt. I had one wish left. This was the big one, right?

"I wish—" I got smacked in the face by a flying stop sign. I rolled, kept rolling. My vision was gone again, and I knew I was on the ground. Everything hurt. I could hear Beth screaming and crying. I peeled open one of my eyes to see the teddy bear's arm detached. There was a mix of fluff and blood spewing from it. It couldn't end like this.

"Don't even *think* of using that last wish," Devil Gabby proclaimed. "You're not even strong enough. You just killed your soul."

I grunted through the pain and put one of my legs under me. Although I didn't feel much different, I did feel slightly lighter. The one leg I got under me was enough to hold my weight for a little longer. I tried to summon the blood-boiled belief I had in the white room. I saw a flash out of the corner of my eye, and suddenly, Beth was hovering just like her mother.

"Don't you *dare* hurt my daddy again!" She screamed and lifted her hands towards the sky. "Don't touch my animals! I command you to give me your power!"

The devil laughed. It pierced through my body like hundreds of tiny knives.

Beth, try again. Believe.

As if she had read my mind, Beth tried again. Her skin was slowly turning white. Whiter than her alabaster skin.

"I command you to die!"

Okay, maybe not that, Beth.

Lucifer continued to laugh and grabbed one of the lightning bolts that appeared near Gabby's left hand, holding it like a small toy, like the God of Thunder, Zeus.

Come on, Beth, try again.

"I command you to be tied up!"

I could see her black eyes. Her hair glowed purple, and her skin looked almost reflective. She looked more angelic than Lucifer, but they both looked insane.

The lightning bolt non-Gabby was holding twisted around her wrist in one swift motion, adorning it like a bracelet. Some force pulled her hand down into the tornado beneath her, and she held the position because of it.

Baffled, the devil let out a snort.

"You think this is going to hold me? For what?"

It looked down at me, and the eye contact was unbearable. I felt like my body was burning up.

"What are you going to do, Swanson? How are you going to

save your precious Gabby? This is just like your father."

My Dad...fought the devil?

"Oh yes, he tried," Lucifer said. I was sure he could hear my thoughts. "I thought I had found the perfect vessel, your mother."

Fuck.

That made sense. I remember hearing them fight about this. Dad needed her to do something for his work, and she opposed it. It was the day before she left. The day before he killed her.

"I tried to make it work. I did." The devil licked his lips, and the snake tongue flicked back and forth. "She wasn't strong enough; she didn't believe. That's when your father stepped in. He offered me a bit of his soul. I killed that bitch the second I had a little control over him."

I remember seeing my Dad in his hospital bed. His death was sudden, but it made sense since everyone said it was liver failure and that son of a bitch drank like there was no tomorrow. It was pretty soon after Tommy's passing. I wasn't even there when he died—I just visited him once when he was first admitted. Apparently the devil works fast.

The cleaver. It's the power.

Raising Gabby's eyebrows, the devil seemed surprised.

"Yes, the cleaver holds the devil's powers. Forged in the blood of slain enemies; however, this time, a cleaver can be created through sacrifices. Ceremonies performed, you can guess the rest. I believe my acquaintance Lent told you. I can choose a vessel whenever, and if you get cut by it—" her eyebrows quickly pointed down, and I was being stared down— "my power is forced into your bloodstream, and I take over."

It cut me. Fuck, can I be controlled now?

"You haven't been cut enough, unfortunately." They laughed again, and I felt like it was bullets this time ripping through me. It was short, but it stung so badly.

"You pathetic humans are useless. I gave them all my wishes, and what did I get? Only hate." This was said through gritted teeth. I could see the facial muscles tensing up. "Even Pisne couldn't control it. He cut himself so much that he ended up bleeding out. For me."

"I CAN'T HOLD MUCH LONGER," Beth yelled at me and snapped me out of this learning game.

It was my time to shine. I had to make that final wish.

All of a sudden, everything stopped.

The devil had transformed into Gabby's physical form, and the air was still there. She floated down, and the street lights grew brighter. I swear there was glitter around her.

Gabby was wearing a blue prom dress—the one from earlier. She had her hair and makeup done. She was gorgeous.

"I can bring her back, you know," Lucifer said in Gabby's voice. "Soft, beautiful Gabby."

She walked over to me, took one of her fingers, and traced my face. My whole body was giving up. I was in so much pain and wanted to give in to the gentle touch. It was so lovely to see her again. But I knew it wasn't her, and I had to do the worst thing imaginable. I had to snap out of this. I had to kill her.

"We can do this together." Gabby gingerly said, tempting me with the 'come here' index finger as she took a few steps back. She was the one trying to take over everyone and everything. Lucifer, craving ultimate power, wanted all of the Wishing Fingers for himself—imagine the life, death, and resurrections you could create. All of the money and power. But on Earth.

Finally, I snapped into the moment. Trying not to think of my plan, I hobbled and followed after her. Mind blank.

"Yes, Justin. My handsome man. I am nothing without you." She lifted her arms as if expecting me to embrace her.

I tried to make my face look like I was trusting her. I saw the future with her; it was hard not to fall into her arms. I was about a foot away from her now. I could almost smell her perfume.

"Fuck you." In between us, I held up my left hand, which only had half of its middle finger left. "I wish for you to fucking die."

Gabby laughed, and this time, it was Gabby's laugh.

"You just killed your precious girlfriend," the devil offered me.

What? Did I wish every part of her to die? Even her soul in purgatory? I thought she could come back, but I remembered the rule. Destroy her physical form completely. It echoed in my head, making me question if I had truly done enough.

You have to destroy her physical form. It echoed in my head.

I looked down, and my finger was starting to disappear. It may have worked.

"I wish for you to die and turn into a single balloon."

"I *command* you to turn into a single balloon." Beth's little voice echoed. She stood next to me and put her small hand on my right forearm. I gave her a half smile.

My finger was lifted in front of my face. A swarm of birds swirled around above us. One by one, they swooped down and took a bite of my finger. Close up, I realized they were bats. They kept coming until my finger was gone.

Lucifer's dress remained, a silent reminder of the supernatural battle. Up in the sky, a single blue balloon floated away.

We did it, but it still didn't feel right. I looked over at Rose's body and could tell she wasn't breathing. She deserved better than this—we all did. I felt my eyes start to water, and before I could stop it, the gates of the tear ducts opened, and a flood poured out of me.

CHAPTER THIRTY-FOUR

I quickly noticed through my tears that I had no more fingers. No other bones accompanied my palms. The purple of my pinky had grown and spread over my left hand. I felt alright, not like I was dying, but also not like I was there. I assumed that, having no fingers and killing my soul, I should be dying by now.

I tried my best and crawled towards Rose to look at her face.

Blood was splattered across her cheeks, and the dent in her head did not look like something she could recover from.

I felt Beth beside me.

"Good job, Daddy," she offered me.

"You too," I answered back.

Where the hell is Gabby?

My tears were still flooding my vision, and I couldn't see much. A bright light started to glow out of Rose's chest.

Please don't look so sad, Swanson. She was talking—her voice—but she wasn't moving her mouth. *It was nice to see you again. Take care of Beth.*

"Where are you going?" I said.

I have to leave now, but my final wish was fulfilled.

She slowly moved her hands so they lay across her body, as if she were hugging herself. The orange color had been rubbed off her pinky. It was green—life.

I guess I have a couple more tricks up my sleeve. I swore she winked and was gone.

I felt awful pain. My hands were stuck inside a shark's jaw, and I could not move. The glow they gave off was blinding, and I looked away. After a good ten seconds, the glowing stopped. I had all my fingers back. Even my pinky nub was gone, and I had a functional digit there. The heaviness of life returned to my body. I couldn't see anything, but I knew my soul was back.

The whisper in the wind said, *"I wish you to live a new normal life after all this."*

I couldn't believe it. What the *fuck* would I do now?

"Let's go home, Beth."

We walked away slowly from the carnage, and as soon as we were clear of it, life seemed to return to normal. People started screaming and exclaiming how messy all this shit was.

How convenient.

We trudged to my old house. Beth was tenderly holding her bear and bat in her arms, trying to nurse the wounds. The other bat that I had wished for turned into another stuffed animal. I can only assume Beth did that. I smiled at the thought that she had taken a wish from me.

I couldn't think of anywhere else to go. I knew the house would be a safe place because it seemed Jeremi had put up all the security and 'fuck off' to anyone who thought of approaching it.

On the way there, Beth and I had a little conversation.

"Where did Rose go?" she asked me.

"She went to a better place, somewhere where angels are." It was the best I could offer her.

"Is that where Mommy is?"

I looked down at her. Feeling the warmth of her hand in mine, I felt like I could answer this.

"Yes, that is where Mommy is."

"Sometimes I can make stuffed animals out of lost people," she said. It seemed like a girl her age would say any random nonsense, but I knew the meaning far too well.

"You could turn Mommy into one if you can find her. Or Rose."

"Okay, Daddy."

The mood was somber. I couldn't bring myself to give her a half smile or tell her everything would be okay. I just found myself in a whole different world. I was now a single dad with no job or income and a stolen house. What the fuck was I doing?

Slowly putting one foot in front of the other, we were again met with the giant chain front door. I opened the door and had the biggest surprise of my life.

Gabby was standing in the entryway in her whole leather outfit. Was she real?

"What the fuck?" I said, forgetting about the kid next to me.

"Well, that's a way to greet someone," she replied.

"How...what?" I was baffled. "I thought only your soul could return."

"I convinced him," she said, motioning to her left. "To resurrect me."

Standing in the kitchen was Lent. He looked ashamed but, at the same time, proud. The suit he wore was faded now; without the blue light, he looked older. He avoided meeting my eyes but did look at Beth, giving a tiny, short smile. How did Gabby have her soul?

I wasn't happy that Lent was here, but I knew that guy had been in the forbidden jello for too long.

"I saved him, so he saved me," she explained. "He was put there because he was trying to stop this all from getting out of hand. Or more so, into Jeremi's hands. Jeremi had other ideas and just locked him up. I freed him from purgatory by wishing his soul back, since I could talk again and bring life. I did one last revival. I consumed one of his fingers. At the same time, he banished me to hell." She looked away. "Lent used his last wish to bring me back. Resurrect me. My energy was then released, and so was he."

Lent held up his hands sheepishly. Once sporting all of his fingers, he now had none.

"I thought *you* were the one who wanted the destruction and Trili to return?" I placed a protective hand on Beth's shoulder. "How the fuck can I trust you?"

Still avoiding my eye contact, Lent let out a short breath.

"I was. I did. It was my idea. I was stuck so long that I never thought I could make it out. I don't know how to say this, but I spent time reflecting on it and seeing you in purgatory with all of your faith for Gabby made me realize that this isn't worth it—not without your father." He sounded sad and remorseful.

I'm glad that bastard is dead as a doorknob.

That was nice, if anything. He did bring Gabby back, though.

"I figured it was about time to use them," he said. "Oh, I also reversed your wish on this house. Good thinking for protecting it for a bit, though."

He laughed, but it was more of a cheerful music box this time. We all knew what was happening.

Beth ran and gave them both a big hug.

"Yay, the whole family is here!" she said, twirling and jumping around.

This little fucker is too sweet. I felt like, in a split second, I had concluded that even if I might not be able to trust Lent fully, it was still really nice to be human and feel so damn lucky.

"Well," I looked at them both. "Now what?"

Gabby smiled and looked at me.

"We become rootin' tootin' fingerless assassins, right?"

"Right," I told her and returned her smile.

"I can get going if you'd like," Lent sounded a little heartbroken. He was starting to fade. A once solid human body was becoming opaque.

"Yeah, get the fuck out," Gabby and I said in unison. Then, we both cracked up. It was so lovely to laugh again and see her. I felt like this was where I belonged.

Not getting the joke, Lent was making his way towards the door. Beth stopped him and looked him up and down.

"I command you to stay," was all she said. She looked up at him, tugging at the tails of his gray suit.

Lent suddenly turned around, finally getting the joke once

he saw our smiling faces, but bent down to Beth's level.

"This world isn't for me anymore," he said tenderly. His whole body looked like mist, glowing a soft pink.

Beth shoved one of her stuffed bats on the floor near him, almost inside of him, and in one swift movement, he funneled into the bat plushy. Beth had a special kind of magic, it seemed.

Baffled, Gabby and I both started laughing awkwardly again.

This was nice, for now.

I brushed Gabby's hand with mine and finally held it for real. My heart skipped a beat as her skin was so soft and familiar that I squeezed out of sheer happiness. She turned to me and placed her hand on my face. She didn't seem to mind that I hadn't shaved in God knows how long or that I was caked in sweat and blood. Her eyes were the brilliant green I remembered them to be, and they glittered just a little. I was melting, and I wanted more. I placed both hands and fingers on her waist and pulled her in for an all-too-familiar kiss.

"Ewwww," Beth let out as she looked away.

We didn't care. We were lost in the moment and kissed as if it were the first time.

CHAPTER
THIRTY-FIVE

In the days following, we cleaned up and tried to resume everyday life. Gabby and I had returned as normal humans, but Beth was our special little angel-devil. She dragged around the lost souls in the stuffed animals and hosted tea parties with them. It was cute, seeing Lent in a little frilly hat with nothing he could do about it.

The house was given back to me as stated in Jeremi's will. I guess he had always had a soft spot for me, as he had left the home to "the previous owner's sons." How fucking kind.

I wanted to remodel it in a way where painful memories wouldn't come up, and I wasn't reminded of Jeremi and his fucked up family. I tried to clean up the pile of rubber ducks, the only remaining traces of Candace. We needed a damn exorcist.

We'd have to figure out what to do with the hands in the weapons closet. It was strange to have all the power to wish but no wishes. The cleavers were lost, and I assumed the watches were, too. At least one was broken. I had another mission.

I called Tommy and let him know what happened. He was

glad everyone was alright. We observed a moment of silence for Rose and dedicated a little plot of land to her soul at Gabby's house. Gabby called Duckie and told him the house was his if he ever wanted to move back.

I would stay in Jersey for a while and hope to fuck that nothing happened again. We had isolated the issue for the time being, but I had a thought about the other bloodlines. Lent said he killed them all off, but what if someone out there found out and wished for Trili to come back? Or created another host for Lucifer?

I hugged Gabby from behind as she cooked dinner, and I felt an overwhelming sense of peace. I inhaled the fresh aroma of garlic and onions cooking and kissed her on the cheek. I turned towards the giant doors of our weapon room. There was only one thing left to do.

We had removed the security system for the time being. Beth was well aware that she was only to handle certain things, and we might eventually renovate it back to storage or a game room. I thought that both Gabby and I were done fighting and swinging axes through people.

So, I retrieved my father's hands from the wall and did everything I could think of.

I put the plaque in a small fire pit at the back of the house to burn, but I had already read it.

"Here are Steven Johnson's hands. A Royal Bearer and the best of the best. May he rest in peace."

I poured some whiskey I found in the cabinet over the hands and tossed a match into the fire. The burn started slowly but then escalated fast. The flames licked the side of the firepit and reached up towards me. They turned into every color I could think of, and then some more.

You set me free, the whisper in the wind said. This time, I knew it was my Dad.

"Good riddance," I said as I turned around and returned to the house.

This isn't over yet, the whisper continued. *I'll find you, Justin.*

I stopped in my tracks.

It was Lucifer's voice.

About the Author

A graduate of Arizona State University with five years of experience in the biotech industry, Ashley is a very creative individual and a first-time author. After years of using writing as an outlet while simultaneously navigating the daily grind of office work, Ashley took a leap to share this little story with the world. When she is not writing, she loves painting, watching movies, and creating resin pieces for her small business. She hopes to publish more stories, along with a poetry book, *Behind Blue Eyes,* soon.

www.ingramcontent.com/pod-product-compliance
Lightning Source LLC
LaVergne TN
LVHW020709110826
845149LV00012B/2183

* 9 7 9 8 9 9 5 6 5 5 8 0 0 *